Team savage

Team savage

from chiraq to slimsonsin

ACE BOOGIE

TEAM SAVAGE

TABLE OF CONTENTS

ACKNOWLEDGEMENTS

I want to thank all the people who believed in me and supported me when everybody else counted me out. Also, I would like to thank my mother, Marguerite Evens Moore, and my mother in law Benitha. Also my first love, Charneese. If it weren't for you, Bagz of Money Content wouldn't exist. To my brothers with whom I was raised, Kutta, K.O., KJ, Slim R.I.P., and Magic for holding me down when I was in them streets. Furthermore, I want to say free the guys, we all crooks, Tre'boi, Big Ryan, Smoody, K.O., Magic, Monte, Lil-T, Smooth, Lil D, Hot Boy, June, Kutta, Nerdo, and Vonn. I want to thank Shawn as well. Last but not least, thank you to all the people who support the game by buying urban novels.

Chapter 1

INTRO

We've been through the storm
We've been through it all
We had some close calls but never would fall
We climbed all the mountains, walked through all the valleys
And you never left me behind.

The beautiful words from Mary J. Blidge song "Stronger" echoed inside Angel's head. She couldn't believe what was happening inside her home. Never in her worst nightmare would she have seen this coming. She laid naked inside the tub with a 9mm pistol resting against her breast. Her mind ran wild and tears ran down her face. How could she leave him behind when he would never abandon her? She felt her heartbeat pounding through her chest from fear. What if he didn't survive? What would she do? Life without him would be agonizing. She struggled to make a decision. Should she stand and fight with him? Or die with him? She clinched the firearm in her hand before saying a prayer to God. It was her responsibility to hold him down. Even if it meant losing her life, she stood to her feet ready to die. Her life flashed before her eyes, memories from the past year invaded her mind. She reviewed the elements of life that brought her to this point.

(3-10-16 FOUR MONTHS EARLIER: MONEY)

It was 8:00 am and Money sat at the door with all his things packed, ready for freedom. "It's time to get your shit and come the fuck on," the corrections officer yelled once count was clear. He couldn't actually believe this day had come. "Be cool, here I come," he commented to the C.O. as he picked his things up and walked out of the room. On his way out of prison, the C.O. was talking about "God knows what." His mind was occupied with getting home to his girl Angel who held him down during his 5-year bid for selling cocaine. The game was decent to Money before the streets caught up with him, putting him in a jam. Money was a 30-year-old trap star with street smarts and knew everything about hustling. He learned the game from being raised on 35th and State in Chicago, Illinois where niggas got laid down left and right. Where it was nothing to see 30 or 40 fiends lining up at any given time of the day, waiting for a fix. He had a twin brother called Cash who he was older than by 15 minutes. They came up in the streets at a young age. Before being knocked, he was able to hide his cash. All the police found were 50 bandz in his crib and seized his cars. There was a half a mill and his house out in Platteville, Wisconsin that no one knew about, not even wifey. He remembered the expression on Angel's face when he said he was broke, the day she came to visit him in jail. She stunned him by saying, "I got you. Imma find a job to take care of us." She knew deep down inside that Money actually was a good person. There was no doubt in her mind that he was the perfect man for her. That's why she was willing to ride this bid out with him regardless of their situation. He lied about being bankrupt because he wanted to test her loyalty. To see if she was down for the team. They'd been together for 10 years. They met when they were 15 years old. Money was the only man she ever loved, but she didn't like his lifestyle. The streets were all he knew. That's where he got his name. He was getting money and was married to the game. He loved the trap so much that at one point he stopped going to school, until Angel got on him about receiving his high school diploma on time. She made sure her man graduated. This was their first time apart. He'd heard stories of niggas leaving a bitch with cash, only to come home broke. He wasn't going let that happen to him. In her heart, he would have turned out different if he had been given a chance. He grew up in the hood in Chicago, and didn't really know his father. His mom moved to Madison, Wisconsin, when he was 14 years old, and by then it was already too late – he was a hoodlum. Violent and brutal, you could've taken him off 35th but you couldn't take the 35th outta him. He was getting kilos by the time he was 18, and turned the fuck up. He spent two years fighting his case and ended up being sentenced to five years in prison. After being down two years, Angel had a degree in Business Management. She'd been working her ass off to take care of them. She made sure he ate, she visited every week, and her phone stayed on for him to call. That's when he finally confessed about the house in Platteville. She wanted to kill him for lying to her and having her work so hard. She understood when he told her it was necessary to make sure she was there for all the right reasons; it was a test and she passed. He was sorry for not believing in her. He wanted her to take the money and split it with his brother Cash. She told him Cash was doing bad. He was running around robbing niggaz, and people were looking for him. The word on the streets was that somebody put 100 Gs on his head, and niggas was try'na see him about that 100 bandz. Every person that didn't have a problem catching a body was on him try'na come up. Money and Cash wasn't close like most twins, and never got along. He didn't wanna see his brother get killed playing games with niggas' paper. It was no problem coming off the cash to see his brother get on his feet. Over the last two years Angel proceeded with business and started Q.O.H. (Queen of Hearts), a strip club in Milwaukee, Wisconsin. Within the last year, Q.O.H. became the hottest club in the state. Showing the importance of education, they were making

$80,000 a month. In Money's mind Angel doing the right thing was a no-brainer, but what shocked him was that Cash used his half to become that nigga in the coke game. He owned Wisconsin streets and was fronting niggas all over the state their work. He moved back to Chicago and put a team of young hitters together. They were killing people left and right on his command. Cash accomplished a lot that he wished he was a part of. Angel said the streets were talking, and Cash was making millions. Money loved the trap; his brother made it, which meant he made it.

The C.O. stopped at the mailroom for him to change into his release fit. Angel made sure he had the best when he walked out the doors. She knew that for a certain type of rich nigga luxury meant comfort, which meant clothes that fit loose, so as not to constrict the swag. Clothes that looked appropriate for watching or even playing sports. She also knew that dressing this way is a power move. It says, "I can get in anywhere without so much as a collared shirt because I'm me." She got him an A.P.C. t-shirt with John Elliot sweat pants, and some common project shoes, making sure he looked like the man in GQ magazine. After changing his clothes, he felt like new money.

"Moore!" the C.O. called, getting his attention. "Your ride is outside." As he approached the last door, his heart began to beat fast, his freedom was only a few steps away. He stepped out of the door and it slammed behind him. He was slapped in the face by the cold breeze from the winter air, which took his breath away. He loved Wisconsin, but the winters weren't something he was accustomed to. He looked up and a delightful site was right in front of him, Angel was standing in front of a Bentley GT. He walked over to her; she had a huge smile on her face. He saw how nervous she was from her leg shaking which she does when she is feeling uneasy. When he made it over, she jumped into his arms, giving him a big hug.

"I'm so happy you're home, Daddy," she said, staring into his eyes before giving him a passionate kiss. He was a lucky man. Angel was any man's dream woman. She was 5'7", big-breasted, and had a fat ass. Everyone always told her she looked like the urban model, Mercedes.

"It's good to be back. Now let's get the fuck outta here," he replied.

"Okay, you drive," she demanded. He slid into the driver seat of the Bentley. The smell of the new leather filled the air inside. Angel hopped into the passenger seat.

"Damn this bitch nice," he said.

"You like daddy?"

"Hell yeah," he said happily.

"Well it's yours. I picked it up last night," she said exposing her adorable dimples. He was too caught up in the beauty of the vehicle to say thanks. The expression on his face was all the thanks she needed. He was fascinated with the fireglow red handcrafted interior and dual tone 3 spoke hide-trimmed steering wheel. This gift outdid anything he'd ever received.

"Where to, Ma?"

"To Milwaukee. I wanna show you yo business," she blurted out.

"Our business," he added. Angel looked at him as he pulled off. She kept smiling; she was so happy at that moment. It was hard for her while he was locked up. Most nights she cried herself to sleep, wishing he could hold her at night. But she waited patiently until he came home. No matter how hard she tried, she couldn't stop the tears from falling. She knew she needed to be strong and hold him down, like he'd done for her. She'd been put through a lot by her father. When she was a kid, he'd get drunk and beat her for the hell of it. He hated her because she reminded him of her mother who left him to raise her on his own. His bitterness caused him to drink, and his drinking made him angry. Most times she ended up with a black eye. The beatings made her shy and weak, which bruised her self-esteem. She never experienced any type of friendship and desperately needed help when she met Money. She still remembered the day like it was yesterday....

(JUNE 16, 2001: ANGEL)

It was 5:30 p.m. She remembered the time because she'd been out looking for her dad. The summer sun was shinning bright, and everyone was enjoying their summer, but not her - she was walking on Todd Drive, headed up the hill to Zimmers Liquor Store to see if he was sitting out front begging for money for a drink. Even though she disliked the way he treated her, she still made sure he was ok. He was all she had, and no matter how fucked up he acted, she loved him because he didn't abandon her like her mother.

"Ay lil mama you need a ride?" Money yelled from a car, breaking her train of thought. She looked up and thought, *damn this nigga fine*, but kept walking, never taking time to respond. She didn't have time for boys and was too shy to say something back.

"Ay Ma, don't act like you don't hear a nigga. What's your name?" he asked, driving along side of her. She looked up and stared into his baby face. He couldn't be any older than her, she thought. The cars behind him honked their horns and went around him, but he wasn't trying to hear that.

"Damn, you ain't gotta be rude Ma, I'm just try'na get you off the side of the road. Why you won't acknowledge a nigga?" he asked casually.

"I'm not try'na be rude, I just don't talk to strangers," she said, never looking his way, and still moving.

"Ok then, I understand that. I'm try'na get to know you. So let me give you a ride." "No," she replied.

"Well, can I walk with you?" he asked, pulling over and parking.

"Yeah, I guess," she said, smiling because most boys would have said fuck her and called her a bitch by now before pulling off. She admired his determination. He wasn't giving up easily. When he stepped out, her heart skipped a beat - he was stunning. She thought it was love at first sight. His dark skin and bright smile took her breath away. His white Ralph Lauren Polo fit was insane, showing his style. Around his neck he wore a dollar sign chain.

He walked up to her and asked, "So you gone tell me your name?"

"Angel," she said, sounding innocent with her head down, unable to look him in his eyes.

"What's down there ma? I'm right here," he said, lifting her chin up forcing her to look at him. He was invading her space making her feel uncomfortable. "You too beautiful to be shy. You know that right?" he assured her, never breaking eye contact as if he was trying to stare into her soul. He grabbed her hand and walked with her without knowing where they were headed. She wanted to pull her hand away but it felt right. They walked in silence side by side without saying anything. Money wasn't normally the shy type, but for some reason he was at a loss for words.

"Ok, this is awkward," she said with a shy laugh.

"Then let's do something about it," he said, flashing his gorgeous smile.

"Like what?" she asked.

"I guess you can stop playing hard to get and give me a chance to get to know you."

"There ain't much to get to know," she said nervously.

"I see you really shy. I'm just gone ask what I wanna know if that's cool," he said.

"I guess that's ok," she responded hesitantly.

"Where you from?" he asked.

"Right here in Madison, what about you?" she asked back.

"The city," he replied like the coolest nigga in the world.

"What city?" she questioned, not understanding.

"Chicago, girl, you green as hell!" he said laughing.

"Oh," she said, putting her head down in shame. She felt dumb. He saw his laughter offended her. The look on her face made him regret laughing, and for some reason, he wanted to protect her. He didn't know anything about this girl, but he felt connected to her. Like it was their destiny to be together. It only took a moment for him to see she was different. He was fascinated that someone this beautiful could be so shy.

"I wasn't laughing at you, I just thought what you said was funny, that's all. We gone have to break you of this shy shit," he said sincerely.

She stopped in front of Zimmers when she spotted her dad's car. Just as she thought - he was there try'na get a bottle. She didn't want Money seeing her dad. He was a disgrace and she was ashamed of him. She hated his drinking and did her best to keep it a secret. He was her father. "Ok I'm here, you can leave."

"You not old enough to drink, what you try'na get outta here?" he asked curiously.

"Nothing. You have to go," she said, looking around scared. She didn't want her dad seeing her talking to a boy in fear of getting her ass whooped.

"So can I get your number?" he asked anxiously.

"I don't have a phone," she replied quickly. He felt something was wrong but didn't know what.

"Damn, you gone use that line on the kid? Ma, you could've said you ain't want me having your number. At least it would've been the truth." She saw the disappointment on his face. The look in his eyes was devastating.

"It's not that I don't want you having my number, you seem cool, but I really don't have a phone." She didn't want him to give up. She wanted a chance to get to know him as well.

"Wait here," Money said, going into Zimmers. He came out two minutes later with a bag in his hand. He pulled out a cell phone and a minute card. "Here, this is for you. Now you won't have an excuse not to call me," he said as he handed her a piece of paper with his number on it.

"I can't take this," she said, surprised and trying to hand the phone back.

"You don't have a choice. I ain't no Indian-giver, and I can't take that back," he announced, firmly putting his hands behind his back.

She smiled. "Ok, thank you." It was the first time anyone other than her father bought her something. His kindness won her heart and from that day on they became inseparable.

(ANGEL)

He was the love of her life. The only man she ever had sex with. From day one, he made her feel comfortable and loved. There was something about his swag that made her go crazy. Money turned Angel out at a young age, which made her fall in love with his sex game. Just looking at him now was making her pussy moist. He was dark skinned with a beard. Dread locks that went to the middle of his back and stood 6 foot 2. Hood nigga was written all over him, just the way she liked. She couldn't wait to see his body after all the years of working out. When they hit the freeway, she said, "I can't wait. I need some of that dick now," and she began rubbing his dick, lustfully giving it a squeeze at the same time. "Can I suck it, Daddy?" she asked, but didn't wait for a reply, already pulling it out of his pants. She got up on her knees on the seat and wrapped her lips around him as he continued to drive. He loved when she took control. Her head game was crazy because she knew what he liked. She licked and kissed his balls. Spitting on his dick and licking it off, driving him wild. "Eat this dick, Ma," he said, grabbing a hand full of her hair, with one hand on the steering wheel trying not to swerve off the road due to the good head he was receiving. She began to rub his dick across her lips and cheek giving it a juicy kiss. "I really missed you," she said talking to it before she took it down her throat making his toes curl. She loved making him feel like a boss, giving him brain in the whip. He was in heaven, and Angel was like a porn star when it came to sex - she would do anything for him. Just sucking his dick after five years took her pussy from moist to super wet real quick. She wanted to fuck him so bad. His dick jumped in her throat.

"I'm about to nut. Make sure you swallow it all, Ma," he said.

Pulling his cock from her mouth, she assured him, "I always do," before putting it back just in time for him to finish. She swallowed every drop giving it a satisfying lick making sure none of it got on him, then putting it back in his pants, sitting back up in her seat. "Don't go straight to the club, Baby. You can see it tonight. At yo coming home party." "How I get to the house in Milwaukee? You know I ain't never been there," he asked. "Just pull over, I'll drive," she said. He pulled over on the highway, and they both switched seats.

They pulled up to the house in Wauwatosa. Seeing the new house blew his mind. It was more than what he expected. In the hood, craftsmanship and quality like this was seldom found. The fabulous custom-built house had 5 bedrooms and 4 baths with hardwood, marble, and granite, and an in-ground pool. The house had to be at least a million dollars. They were doing well, but a million on a house, shit wasn't that decent.

"How much was this house?" he blurted out.

"2 mill," she said like it was nothing.

"Is it paid for?" Money asked. Angel knew he didn't like being in debt.

"Yes, it's paid for," she said.

"Ok, how much we got in the bank?" She displayed a shocked expression when he asked this question, showing something was wrong.

"120,000," she replied. To Money that wasn't shit, but still he felt immaculate about where they were in life.

"You did good, Ma," he said, putting a smile on her face. She perceived he would say something inappropriate. They were legit now with a business and a place to call home. He liked the feeling of living without worrying about going back to jail. The only thing better than being ghetto fabulous was being legit and fabulous.

He hopped out of his car and ran to open the driver's door for his queen. "Thank you," she said. Angel loved the attention he was showing her. She went too long without him being there. She was happy that he was home because, at times, she was weak and being alone was very hard for her. Even though she seemed to have her shit together. Angel was still only human so she needed companionship, but she would never step out on him with another man. He was a real nigga, and she only enjoyed his company. He was the only man she was actually interested in. While he was away, she made a mistake and cheated on him with a woman. The worst part was that Angel had fallen in love with her. She planned on telling him, but didn't know where to begin. Before he went away, he was her only lover. She was scared he might look at her different. She didn't want to be seen as a slut. Angel didn't know how she gotten into this situation. "Angel, you coming?" he yelled once he made it to the house and she was still standing by the car. "Yeah," she said, running to meet him with the key. She opened the door, letting him in. As soon as they got inside, he attacked her with kisses before taking her in his arms. She really missed sex and was addicted to his love. Her pussy was so wet; she broke the kiss, grabbed his hand, and led him to the bedroom. He pulled her close again, kissing her neck and whispering in her ear, "I been waiting to do this five years." "Then, I know you going to beat the pussy up," she replied, real sexy. He laid her down on the bed, never breaking their kiss. He put his hands under her shirt to take her bra off to find out she wasn't wearing one. He started playing with her nipples knowing it drove her insane.

As he was running his tongue down her stomach, she said, "Stop playing, I want the dick." She'd been getting her pussy eaten and had enough of that, now she wanted to be fucked.

"I'm going to lick this pussy first," he told her, before pulling off her jeans. She lifted her hips as he pulled them off, also removing her panties. The immaculate smell of her fragrance filled the room. He stopped and took in her body. Then started to run his tongue along her fat pussy, sucking on her clit making her jump and squeeze her legs around his head.

"Stop baby, fuck meee," she asked seductively, but he didn't listen and instead he inserted two fingers in her pussy.

"Stop, fuck me," she begged and pleaded.

"Say please, tell me you want this dick," he said.

"I want Daddy's dick please." He pulled his two fingers out and put them in her mouth.

"How that taste, Ma?" he asked as she licked his finger clean.

"Delicious Daddy."

His dick jumped from her tasting her own juice, he loved that freaky shit. As he began to take off his clothes, Angel couldn't help but to embrace his body and big dick. He got on top of her and started sliding his hard, throbbing dick into her wet pussy.

"Oh my God, it's soooo thick," she quenched up. "Go slow." Money put his hands around her waist and slowly pulled her forward sinking his dick into her wet pussy as the space between them closed. Angel wrapped her arms and legs around him squeezing him close. Surrendering her body to him completely, she gasped loudly as he flexed his hips. He began pulling in and out of her with long, powerful strokes as her pussy stretched out from his size.

"Damn, yo pussy the best," he moaned.

"Daddy, it's too much," she said as her mouth fell open in pleasure and pain.

"It's yours, right? This yo dick?" Angel was so out of control with passion and excitement that she answered Money's questions, blurting out between moans and sighs

"Oh God, yes!" Since he had just nutted, he was able to hold out a lot longer this time.

"Then take it," he said with bass in his voice.

She became used to his size. "Like this, Daddy?" she asked, throwing her pussy at him.

"Yeah, just like that," he said, beginning to go full throttle. He was beating her pussy up, and for a moment she couldn't say a thing. The dick was taking her breath away; it was so proper. A tear ran down her face.

"You ok? " he whispered when he saw her tears.

"Yesss, you just fucking me sooo good," she assured him. With everything being good, he picked up where he left off and she exploded on his dick. Even before she climaxed, he was half way to his nut and he discharged inside her. They lay there spent from the pleasure. Angel got up to make Money something to eat, and he went to take a shower.

(CHICAGO)

It was a cold day in the Windy City. The wind could be heard as it blew passed your face. The streets were empty except for a group of men on the corner, rocking back and forth and try'na stay warm. Running up a check was the only thing on their minds other than the weather. Even though it was wartime, they weren't worried about the BDs. A block up the street sat two killaz in a stolen Audi.

"These niggas think shit sweet," June said to his little brother. Killa sat behind the wheel, smoking a blunt. He shook his head at how hard they were lacking. He felt like they were being disrespected, by them having the nerves to try to hustle, like they didn't just kill his homie a week ago. They sat back waiting for the perfect opportunity to make their move.

"What they forgot? We shoot all day and all night," Killa said, passing the blunt. June hit it twice, inhaling the smoke before blowing it out.

"Mutha fuckas ain't forgot shit bro. These niggas just don't give a fuck," he took another pull before continuing.

"A nigga gotta eat. Wartime or not."

"Then make em eat a bullet bro," Killa said, laughing at his own joke. June took a sip of lean try'na get in the zone.

"Ay, bro, if I'm lacking like this," he said pointing his fingers at the GDs before continuing, "and it's wartime, do me a favor and lay me down. Don't let an opp add me to they body count." June laughed at his brother. He was one of David's finest. If the old man were still alive, he'd love the young nigga. June tried to keep his eyes open on the block. Waiting to see a hype come through to make his move. But shit was moving slow out there. It was so cold the hypes were laid up.

"This block slow as hell," Killa said reading June's mind.

"I know, right? It's cool though, we ain't got shit better to do. On the low, I'm try'na get paid for bodying one of these niggas," June said.

Their boss, Cash, had five bands on any of their heads. He was try'na put pressure on them to buy his product. June didn't give a fuck what Cash's agenda was. He did it to feed his team. Anything else wasn't his business. If a nigga had money on his head, he was try'na collect, no questions asked.

"Ya, I could use a few dollars too," Killa added.

"I ain't gone lie to you, lil bro, I been doing a lot of thinking about opening up the block around the corner. To move some work," June said, sipping from his cup.

"Bro, you know Cash ain't having that shit. You a hitter on the team, not a hustler. You know like I know that's against the rules." As Killa finished his sentence, a van pulled up. The whole crowd took off running to the car with their backs to the streets.

"Right now, lil bro," June said, his eyes beyond wide giving Killa the okay to pull up. He sat up in his seat with the blunt hanging from his mouth. He pulled up and slowed down, June got out and left the door open. The hustlers was to busy try'na make a swerve. When June got close enough, he aimed his .40 at the crowd with a two-hand grip like the police.

Bloc! Bloc! Bloc! Bloc! Bloc! Bloc! Bloc! Bloc! Bloc! Bloc!

By the time they realized what happened, bullets had danced up two of their backs, knocking them to the ground. Some of them took off running as he continued to fire.

Bloc! Bloc! Bloc! Bloc!

Unable to hit anyone else, he ran up to the bodies on the pavement. He noticed the driver's head laying against the steering wheel and blood on the passenger window. There was a hole in his temple. He stood over one of the wounded men and shot him in the back of the head. Bloc! His head exploded and blood sprayed onto June's Jordans. He kicked the other nigga in the ass.

"Turn over, Pussy!" June yelled. He flipped over and mean mugged June, spitting up blood.

"Tell David we out here taking over when you get to hell," June said smiling.

"Fuck David, Pussy!" the dying man shouted.

"What!" June said, putting the pistol to the man's forehead, blowing his brains out. Bloc!

He ran back to the car, and Killa casually pulled off. Passing the blunt back to his brother as if nothing happened.

"Now what was you saying, June?" Killa asked.

"Oh, I'm try'na get paid," he said, laying back in his seat with his .40 on his hip.

Chapter 2

MONEY

Once he got out of the shower, he thought about how much he loved his new home. It was beautiful with an open floor plan for fabulous entertaining. He went downstairs to get something to eat. When he came into the kitchen with its new stainless steel appliances and elegant hardwood floors, his heart dropped at the sight of Angel wearing a pair of boy shorts and a wife beater. Her ass looked great, and Money's dick jumped when he walked behind her, smacking it before taking a seat. He felt great being free. After five years in prison, it felt good not being told what to do. Also, he was elated that his days of smelling another man's shit were behind him. Just being able to smack his girl's backside was a joy. He took the time to admire her nice butt as she made his plate. She popped her cheeks one at a time, then turned around, catching him staring.

"You like what you see?" she asked, licking her lips and grabbing a handful of her ass.

"Ya, Ma."

"Well you can get it any time you want," she said, walking over, dropping between his legs, and rubbed his cock through his boxers. It hardened, then she stopped, and went to get his food, leaving him with a hard dick.

"That's how you gone do yo man?" he asked.

"Boy, you had enough," she said and brought him his plate. She sat down to watch him eat.

"Damn, this shit good, Bae," he said.

"Boy, you know I can cook," she said with dislike in her eyes but a smile on her face. She stood up and rubbed his back as he ate, treating him like a king.

"So what's up with Bro? Give me his number so I can hit him up." Angel knew this would happen. She didn't wanna to tell him that late last night, his brother stopped by with the 250 bandz he borrowed him, telling her to enlighten Money that he wasn't fucking with him. The only reason he was paying him back was that he didn't want to owe him shit.

"Bae, don't get mad but your brother stopped by last night and dropped off yo money. He told me to tell you thanks for the little loan, and he knows you needed it back. He was jacking talking about he don't want to see you fucked up." His expression changed to confusion.

"What?" he managed to utter. "What the fuck is that suppose to mean?" he asked with frustration. Angel hated being the bearer of bad news.

"Bae, he said he ain't fucking with you, until you remember he hot. He said you should know what that meant." Money's mind was all fucked up. Cash was holding onto a grudge over some old shit. He sighed.

"Well fuck that nigga then," he said out loud, more to himself than to her.

"I know you don't need him. You got me, and I'm gone always hold you down. I got, I got, yo back boy," she said, singing the hit Keri Hilson sang. He couldn't help laughing at her crazy ass. She always knew what to say at the right moment.

"Come here," he motioned for Angel as she grabbed his hand and he pulled her on his lap. The feeling of her soft bottom was getting him hard again. Angel didn't make it any better thrusting her hips back in forth and a wonderful rocking motion trying to turn him on.

"You gone finish what you started?" Money asked, rubbing her clit through her boy shorts, tracing it with his finger as he kissed the back of her neck. She began breathing deeper and heavier. He had her and his clutches and was enjoying every minute.

"We gotta get to the club," she said, laying her head on his shoulder. She wanted him so bad right now, but it was his turn to play with her. He stood up and bent her over the table, she stuck her ass out ready to get fucked. He smacked it and walked off.

"You ain't the only one who can play games," he said, walking out of the kitchen leaving her with her ass in the air.

"Daddy, stop playing!" she yelled, crying out for him, but he was already halfway to their room, smiling from getting the best of her.

"You play too much," she whined, following him, jumping on his back, hitting him playfully. It was moments like this that he missed all them years in a cell. He threw her on the king size bed. Angel laid there wishing he'd fuck her again, but now wasn't the time. Money looked at her and thought she was gorgeous. She'd become a woman while he was away. When they first me, she was a little rough around the edges. He knew she was the one for him the moment he first laid eyes on her.

"We gotta go to the club, Daddy," she said, opening her legs, inviting him in. He didn't have a problem invading her space, and she wrapped her legs around him.

"Let me get my mind off this muthafucker Cash and then we gone head out," he responded, kissing her.

"Wait, let me get this correct, you between my thighs, thinking about yo brother?" Angel asked, playfully pushing him off her, and standing up.

"My bad, Ma," he laughed.

"Don't worry, Daddy, I know you hurt, I'm just try'na take yo mind off it," she lied.

"Whatever, you try'na get this dick, that's it," he said, smiling.

"Boy, whatever. Imma bout to take a shower," she said, going in the bathroom. Money sat on the bed thinking. He couldn't get over the fact that his brother tried to play him. He loved a challenge and planned to show Cash who was the boss. When he got out the joint, he knew he was getting back in the game, but he wasn't going to rush it. When the time was right, he'd know it. His plan had been to just fall back and sell weight with his brother. But Cash ended that before it even started. It was essential to come up with something different, he needed to mentally reshape all his ideas. The difference between him and the average nigga was that Money was street smart. He analyzed everything and was knowledgeable in every aspect of the game. His brother let him down, but it wouldn't stop him. He knew what it felt like to be disappointed by someone you loved. Cash cut him so deep, he was sure he wouldn't trust another nigga again.

(CASH)

Cash was in Chicago taking in the city, riding around with no set destination. He was in his so-called low-key trap car, a $90,000 Land Rover Range Rover TDB. He switched lanes just for the hell of it, going 100 miles an hour. Even though it was wartime, he had to get his shine on. Ever since he became the man in Wisconsin, he was hardly there. He knew better than to spend his money where he made it. He attempted to stay low when he hit the streets, but clearly he did not know the meaning of low-key. He was coming from downtown after buying a new outfit for Money's coming home party. He was only going in order to broadcast that he made it on his own. Or at least that's how he viewed it. He had a lot of spite in his heart for his brother. He spent three years running the streets, robbing and killing, just to escape with shoe money while his big bro was holding out the whole time . He put in a lot of work for that money as well. Before his brother's dilemma, they used to be partners. Cash and his team pushed niggas off the block, and Money did all the trapping, moving the work until they fell out, splitting up the team. When Angel called him with the money, he didn't feel grateful. His first thought was "about time." He wasn't a hater, but was happy that things played out the way they did with Money getting locked up. He took the 250 bandz from Money and made it happen, taking over the cocaine business, and in just over two years, he was worth $10 million. In his heart there was no thanks to Money, he'd succeeded on his own. His mentality was "fuck Money." He wasn't welcoming him home. His reason for attending the party was to stunt on his brother. He sped up the city streets reckless, letting the money go to his head and forgetting about family. The bass pumped from his speakers as he rapped along with Lil Durk. Life was good, he thought as he glided down the city streets.

He pulled up on 24 and Lamron to meet up with his young hitter, June. This young boy was something else, it's like he was born to murder. At eighteen, he already had 10 bodies under his belt. He wasn't showing any sign of letting up. His younger brother, Killa, wasn't far behind him on the body count. Growing up, they never knew their father, so that saying "a woman can't raise a man" was far off in their case because their OG raised two savages.

When he pulled up, he spotted 15 young D-boys posted up. Everyone was watching his Range Rover on 24s. Future's "Never Be The Same No More" was bumping through the speakers.

"Yeah my glasses from Germany, designer on me permanently, these scars on me permanently, this pain is ahh burnin me. But it ain't killing me, its boostin up my energy. I'm on my way to Tennessee, doing a show for 10 a key." He rapped along with Future as he parked. All eyes were on him just the way he preferred. He hopped out wearing a black and red Chicago Bulls snapback, an all black Louis Vuitton jacket, black Levi's jeans sagging just enough that you could see his Louis Vuitton belt, and his black and red Jordan Number 3s fresh out the box. It was cold as hell out there, but niggas was still out. The show didn't stop just because it was winter. He left the engine running, wishing a nigga would try him. His young boy was always ready to murk something. He walked up to the crowd and shook up with everybody. June sat at the top of the stairs behind everybody, smoking a blunt. As Cash walked up the stairs, he heard young Killa commanding niggas to be on point while big folks was here. They started going to corners to guard the block. He loved this shit, there was nothing like being successful.

"What's good, Skud," June said, putting his hand out to shake up. They did the clink fist handshake before June passed him the blunt. Cash took a seat next to him.

"Shit, Skud, came to see what y'all niggas on," he said taking a pull from the blunt and holding it in.

"Man, you the only rich nigga I know that wanna hang in the hood. If I was you I would've left and never looked back," June chuckled, shaking his head. He didn't understand Cash at times.

"Nah, that ain't real nigga shit, Skud, you can't forget where you came from. I come out here to remind me where I used to be. It keeps me from forgetting the struggle and pain," he said, taking a pull from the blunt and passing it back to June.

June hit the loud saying, "Ya that's real, I'm feeling that, Skud." Cash reached in his pocket pulling out 10 bandz and handed it to June.

"This that money from them two bodies you dropped for me earlier." June put the money in his jacket.

"Good looking, Skud. That's right on time," he said, passing the blunt back to Cash before calling Killa.

"What's good, Bro?" Killa asked. Killa was a skinny nigga around 6'1" with a low cut and 360 waves. He wasn't a pretty boy like his brother but he still had hoes.

June counted out 5 bandz before handing it to him. "Give every one of the guys 350, and when you done I got 2,500 for you."

"Cool bro," Killa said, calling his niggas over and passing out the money.

"Damn nigga, you just gave away 7,500. You should be stacking that shit," Cash said.

"You right, Bro. But when I eat, I make sure we all get a plate. These my day one niggas. We grew up together, we used to go half on sacks with each other, eat out each other's cribs when we didn't have food. We family so everything I got, they got," he said sincerely.

"I feel that my nigga," Cash said, standing up. He shook up with him, hopped in his car, and pulled off. He liked June's style, he was a real nigga across the board. He turned up his music listening to Chief Keef "Ballin." *Rollin' up this dope, pop a nigga something like Driscoll, all I do is spend dough, I don't even know these bitches know mo cuz I'm ballin',* he rapped along, leaning back in his seat vibing to the music. He pulled up on 63rd and King Drive in the back of the parkway buildings to purchase some loud from his niggas and 16oz of lean to sip on. He reverse parked so he could see everything moving in the lot. He pulled out his Desert Eagle and laid it on his lap. Even though he was well-respected down here, it wouldn't stop a nigga from trying him. Shit, niggas got killed every day down here. He called his man, informing him that he was out back. Five minutes later, his guy came out, climbed through the hole in the gate, and then got in the passenger side of the car.

"What's good, B?" Cash said, holding out his hand to shake up.

"You already know my nigga, try'na get like you," Bull said, shaking up. He handed Cash the ounce of loud and the drink.

"Ya whatever, nigga, I'm trying get like you," Cash joked as he pulled out 10 bandz, counted off 500, and gave it to him.

"I see you on some funny man shit," Bull laughed, putting the money in his pocket. "When you gone stop playing and hit a nigga with some of them bricks?" Bull added.

"When you stop playing and prove you want some real paper," Cash replied, laying back in his seat and rolling up a blunt. Bull was his man, but the nigga was a fuck-up. He always tried to live above his means. Bull was the type of nigga with 5 bandz in his pocket but living like he had millions, spending everything and always falling off hard.

"Ya, you right, Skud, I do need to get it together," Bull said, keeping it hot.

"Ya you do, Bro, cause you plug in with the man. But a nigga can't trust you with the work. I got mad love for you too Bro, that's why I don't hit you off. "I'm not try'na go to your funeral, you feel me," Cash said, keeping it real with his mans.

"Ya, I feel you Bro, but let me get outta here before 12 come," Bull opened the door and hopped out.

"Love boy," Cash yelled before pulling off. On his way up King Drive, he flamed up his blunt. At the lights, an all white Rolls Royce with tinted windows pulled up next to him. He took a draw from his blunt and admired the car. They were doing him in that muth-fucka. He wished he would've brought out his Bentley Bentayga. It wasn't fucking with the Rolls Royce, but it would've been a better look than the Range Rover. The window rolled down and Chief Keef was smoking a blunt. When the light turned green, he sped off. Cash smiled and thought about how he just flexed on him. It was cool though, he was gone step it up this summer and fuck the whole city up. He pulled up to a gas station, and ran in, grabbed a Sprite, a cup of ice, and some Jolly Ranchers, then paid before leaving. It was time to pour up. He had second thoughts about playing his twin the way he planned, but quickly neglected the thought, pushing it to the back of his mind. He took into consideration the three years he spent struggling while Money was sitting on half a million in cash. Now it was his time to get reparations.

(ON THE BLOCK)

The room was full of smoke, there was 15 niggas passing blunts around trying to warm up from being in the streets. They sat on anything that could hold weight. June looked around and saw his guys looking like bums compared to Cash. He thought about Cash pulling up in a car that cost more than their houses.

As the leader of his team, he felt like a failure. It was up to him to make sure they ate. He stood up and locked his fingers together over his chest in a D-Boy stance. Everyone stop what they were doing, putting out the blunt to talk nation business. They stood up and locked their fingers together over their chest as well. They became silent, giving June the floor.

"I wanna open this prayer with a lot of love to the king of all kings. King David. Our crown king, King Shorty, in all righteous black disciples of the world. We are strong, we are stronger together, my love and yours forever." June finished the rest of the prayer, then addressed the crowd.

"I know everybody in here remember that prayer. But do everybody understand it? Like really, really, understand the words that's being said? Because if y'all do, y'all know we are stronger together," he said, pausing for a second to let the words sink in.

"I know y'all feel like me, because I know we think alike. We been at this shit too long. We been guys since day one. No homo, but I love y'all niggas. But we gotta change how we living. Look at us bro, we look like bums. But we gone fix that, don't worry." Every person in the room agreed with him.

"I know some niggas in here got a few dollars saved up. But what good is having a few dollars when we could have millions. We about to get ours by any means. If a nigga ain't in this room, he ain't with us. Before the end of this week, we gone open up a spot down the block." He looked around at all the good niggas in attendance. Everybody around was stomp down killas and only a few was hustlers.

"Y'all know like I know, Cash ain't gone be feeling our movement. Y'all know what I'm saying. This breaking a big rule of his. So we gotta keep this shit between us." No one said anything, so he continued.

"I need everybody to go home and grab any money they can afford and bring it to the spot." Before they left, he blessed the meeting with a lot of love to their fallen kings.

Twenty minutes later, everybody made it back. The money added up to 15 bands. Most of it was the 10 bands he made today, and 5 bands came from Tre Boi and Big Ryan. It wasn't looking too good, but it would have to do. He had a connect who would give him some work without Cash knowing. He grabbed the money and left. As soon as he stepped outside, the wind blew his hood off his head. His dreads blew in the wind. He hopped in his 2004 Monte Carlo, started the engine up, and pulled off. It didn't take him long to pull up to Sharks. When he walked in, T-Mack was behind the counter frying wings. He was a major hustler in Cash's organization. Once he saw June, his face lit up and a smile crossed it.

"What's good, B?" he yelled, coming to the door that separated the employees from the customers, letting June in the back.

"Shit, my nigga," June said, shaking up with him. "I need to rap with you real quick," he continued.

"Aight, step to the back," he replied taking off his apron. June followed him to his office. A flat screen and sofa sat in the corner. T-Mack closed the door behind them and took a seat.

"What's good?" he asked, picking up the remote and turning to the game. June took a seat next to him. He pulled the bands from his pocket and put the stack on his lap.

"I need a favor, Bro," June said, getting to the point.

"What's good?" T-Mack said, rolling his eyes. He had love for June like a little brother, but he was always up to some bullshit.

"Damn, that's how you feel, Bro?" June asked, hearing the aggravated tone in his voice.

"Naw, it ain't like that. What's good, Lil Bro?" T-Mack said, try'na hear him out.

"Aight. I got 14 bands right now, I'm try'na get you to front me a brick." T-Mack put his head back and took a deep breath. Some shit never changed, he thought. June wanted him to go against his boss's orders. A nigga that fed his family.

"So you want to go against the code? Come on Bro, that shit could get me killed," he said, rubbing his face.

"Bro, you known me how long? Come on Nigga, you know my mouth duct-taped. I won't make a sound. Cash will never know about it, that's on David."

"Damn, June, I got you," T-Mack said, knowing June was a man of his word.

"Good looking, Big Bro," June said, counting off a band and putting it back in his pocket. He gave T-Mack the rest of the money, and T-Mack got up and went to get the bird. June tucked it in the front of his pants before pulling his shirt down.

"Be careful," T-Mack said and led the way out. June hopped in the car and made the short drive to the block. He put the brick in his mom's house, then went to the hardware store. He picked up some boards and six 2x4s to put on the doors. After that he got some food stamps from a hype and picked up 2oz of loud. He spent over $500, but it would save him money in the long run. Once everything was set, he went home to get some rest. He needed some sleep to attend Cash's brother's coming home party tonight.

Chapter 3

MONEY, 12.00 A.M.

*T*he interior of the club was flooded with people, naked strippers were dancing around try'na make a wage giving lap dances. The neon lights flashed everywhere, and when a big spender strolled in, the DJ shouted them out, informing everyone they were in the building. Money was installed at a table, inside Q.O.H. he couldn't help feeling like a general. He changed his clothes before coming out. He was wearing all white Louis Vuitton from head to toe. His shoes alone cost damn near a band. The club was packed with people he didn't know, but a lot of niggas from Madison came down to show love. Most folks didn't know it was a coming home celebration for the owner. They were just try'na have a good time and enjoy the drinks. A song by G.B.E. was playing which turned Money up. When he was in jail, he heard about the young BDs taking over the Midwest music world. Being inside the club for the first time, he was finally able to see what Angel accomplished, and he was proud of her. Tonight was the most important night and as an elite organization, Q.O.H always received the new music before any other club. They had the finest females from all over the state and out of Chicago. He was having a great time, but still couldn't take his mind off Cash try'na play him. But he wasn't a hater, he was happy Cash found his way in the game. Tonight he was going enjoy himself, then it was back to business.

(MEANWHILE AT Q.O.H.)

Angel and Kia sat in Angel's office. Kia was the woman Angel couldn't get enough of. They'd become lovers while Money was doing time. Kia knew he was on his way home. She'd been looking forward to it. She loved the stories Angel shared with her about how certified he was in bed. She wanted a chance to feel him inside of her.

"Girl, all you gotta do is tell him, he ain't gone give a fuck, what man don't want two bad bitches in his life?" she said giggling. Angel was scared to confess what happen between them.

"Girl, Imma tell him, just not tonight." Angel stood up to glance out her office window, she could see the entire club through the picturesque glass window that provided a great view of the nightclub. Money was still seated in the VIP having drinks back to back by himself. She couldn't help how much she loved him, and she wanted to confess everything. Kia walked to the custom bar positioned in the corner. She poured Angel a double shot, hoping to ease her nerves. Kia came up behind her and hugged her and kissed her neck. The kiss made Kia's mind slip back to the day she met Angel.

It was a nice summer night when Kia reported to work at Q.O.H for the first time. A week ago she auditioned and got the job. She wished she didn't have to do this, but she didn't have a choice. Things were hard on her right now, and she was broke. Kia was a trap queen. She did whatever necessary for the paper. She sold dope, robbed, and sometimes stripped. She was short on cash and couldn't find a lick. She thought about visiting an old friend for help, but didn't want to sink down to fucking him for money. And even though what she was about to do wasn't much better, at least she didn't have to give up any ass. After going to Q.O.H. to get a job as a stripper, she met Angel her first night there, in the same place they were in now. Angel was giving her the run down on what was expected of her on the job. Kia felt attracted to Angel from day one. She'd been in a relationship with a man, but couldn't find happiness. Most niggas wasn't real enough for her, and she always end up leaving their lame asses. About two years previous, she decided to date women, and she loved it. There was nothing like the soft touch of a woman. She loved the feeling she got while in control of her mate. Angel and Kia hit it off, becoming friends over the next five months. They hung out almost every day and talked about everything, even how many sex partners they had. Kia made passes at Angel, but she always turned her down, until one night she gave in, while in the club having drinks.

"Girl, guess who been try'na talk to me with his ugly ass?" Angel asked, folding her arms over her chest.

"Who bitch?" Kia replied, taking a sip from her drink .

"J.R.'s lame ass from the south side, bitch. I don't know what I did that made his black ass try me, like I'm some bum ass bitch," Angel said, her face plastered with disgust.

"Bitch, you know it's always them bum ass niggas that be quick to step to a bad bitch like they the shit," Kia said, rolling her eyes.

"Girl, yo ass crazy. I never noticed that shit, but it is true though," Angel added, spinning around.

She called the bartender over and told him to give them two more shots of Louie 13. They'd been sipping on the best all night for free, one of the benefits of owning a bar. When he came back with the shots, they downed them. Kia was feeling good and started feeling herself.

"Ya bitch, that's why you need to leave that dick alone and let me suck yo pussy," she commented seductively, while staring into Angel's eyes. Over the last five months, Kia found herself falling for Angel. There was something about being turned down that really turned her on. Ever since becoming a lesbian, she used and abused women's bodies like so many men had hers. One of the reasons she became a lesbian was her love of control. But Angel was different and she found herself falling in love.

"Here you go with that bullshit again, Girl. I don't know how many times I'm gone tell you, this pussy only for my man," Angel said, playfully putting her finger in her face. Kia put it in her mouth and sucked on it like she would've suck her clit. She was surprised when Angel didn't pull away. If she didn't know better, she saw lust in her eyes.

She drew her lips away before saying, "How many times I'm gone tell you yo nigga could care less about you letting a woman eat yo pussy. It's every man dream to have a threesome." Angel's clit begin to throb as she thought about her fantasies to have a threesome. The reason she didn't stop talking to Kia was the idea of messing with a woman. Something about it turned her on, but she wasn't ready to act on it.

"Girl, stop it with that shit, I ain't try'na go there with yo crazy ass tonight," Angel said, ending the conversation. Kia didn't want to push her away, so she let it go. She valued their friendship more.

"You need to keep an eye on that nigga JR, bitch, because he known for taking some pussy. You got a crazy one on yo hands," Kia said, putting her girl up on game.

After a long night of drinking, Angel was feeling no pain as she walked to her car. When she opened the door, someone came up behind her.

"Don't move bitch or Imma kill you," she heard somebody say and felt a knife press to her neck, frightening her.

"I got money, just take it, please don't kill me," she pled.

"I don't want yo money, bitch, I want this pussy," he whispered, gripping her fat ass.

"Please don't do this, JR," she said as tears ran down her face.

"Get in, bitch," he belted, striking her in the back of the head and pushing her inside the car. She wasn't about to let him rape her without a scuffle. She kicked him trying to fight him off and began screaming for help. Kia came rushing out of the club trying to run Angel down because she'd left her phone at the bar. When she stepped outside, she saw JR on top of Angel, beating her. She pulled out her knife, ran over, and jumped on his back. She pulled him off Angel, stabbing him in the back.

"Shit!" he yelled in pain. Before she could stab him again, he slammed her against a car knocking the wind out of her. Kia fell to the ground with the knife still in hand. JR kicked her in the face.

"Bitch, you stabbed me!" he said, angrily kicking her again. Angel wasn't a fighter, but she went crazy seeing him kick Kia. She grabbed a handful of his afro and yanked his head back, using her free hand to claw his face. Kia was dizzy but she got to her feet as JR punched Angel, knocking her to the ground. His back was to her, so she stabbed him again, this time in his ear. He fell to the ground shaking. She pulled the knife from his ear and looked at him as he died. This wasn't Kia's first time taking a life, but she wasn't numb to it. She found herself in shock. Angel looked at Kia spacing out and grabbed her.

"Come on, Girl, we gotta go." She tugged her to the passenger side and helped her in. Angel stepped over JR's body, got into the car, and pulled off. By the time they arrived to Angel's house, Kia had snapped out of it and returned to normal. Only for Angel to fall apart and become a mess. She was crying her heart out.

"We going to jail," she said, shaking and thinking about what took place. Kia looked at her. She couldn't believe this bitch was crying over a nigga that tried to rape her.

"He attacked you! I did what I had to. Ok girl! And we can't tell nobody about this. We gotta keep it between us, you understand?" Kia asked, holding Angel's face trying to calm her down.

"Do you understand we had to? Look at your face, girl. He was going to kill you. I couldn't let that happen, you understand me?" Kia said softly.

"Yes," Angel replied. The way Kia took control of the situation was calming her down and turning her on at the same time. It reminded her of Money and how long she had been alone. Kia wanted her so bad, but up until tonight, Angel wanted her to cut it out. It wasn't that Kia wasn't sexy. She was 5'8" and about 150 pounds with an amazing body equipped with 34C breasts with a 30-inch waist. Her weight was in all the right places. She was light skinned and had these sexy brown eyes. Angel glanced into her eyes and felt safe. Her man had been gone for three and a half years, and she was horny as hell. Kia saw the expression on Angel's face. Kia gave her a hug and as she leaned in, Angel kissed her. She was surprised, but enjoyed it, which lead to them having sex. Over time Kia fell in love with Angel. Kia was the kind of person that loved deep. There wasn't a better person in this world for her. The way they made love was crazy. She'd never cum so much in her life. Angel could easily turn anyone out.

"He's sexy, isn't he?" Angel asked, bringing Kia outta her flashback.

"Yeah he is." Money was down in VIP having his own little party, and you could tell he was glad to be home.

"Imma go be with my boo, it's his night," Angel said, turning around kissing Kia on the lips before heading out the office.

(1:00 A.M. CASH)

Cash walked into Q.O.H. with Robins on and four chains around his neck. His dreads were pulled back into a ponytail hanging down his back. He had 20 young niggas behind him all between 18 and 20 years old. They were reckless, young, and had something to prove, that's why he kept them around. He turned his swag up walking through the club. All eyes were on him and his young boyz. Everyone wondered who the unknown people were walking through the club this deep.

The DJ came over the speaker, "Ah shit, ladies get ready to make some real paper, my muthafucken man Cash just walked in the building. What it do my nigga?" he shouted. Cash threw the tres up and kept it moving, acting like he was Obama or something. The women in the club whispered to each other wondering who was going home with him tonight. Cash walked over to the bar and a female bartender came rushing over stepping to him at the counter.

"How may I help you?" she asked, smiling.

"I need a table, 20 bottles of Ace of Spades, and 20 bottles of peach Ciroc." The bartender's demeanor changed from the large order.

"Ok, I'm gone show you to your table, and then I have to talk to the owner about your order," she said.

"Look, lady, I'm good for the money, that ain't shit to me," he said, annoyed. He looked at his Rolex showing her she was wasting his time.

"I wasn't trying to offended you, it's standard procedure that we talk to the owner about large orders," she said before leading the way toward the VIP section. It was extremely crowded in the club and his hitters pushed niggas and bitches aside for him to get through. They finally made it to their table and got seated. Cash watched the bartender make her way over to a table where Angel and Money were seated. She began to talk to them, and then Angel pointed towards Cash's direction. She nodded her head "yes" and the bartender ran off. Ten minutes later, 10 people came to their table holding golden colored buckets of champagne and set them in front of them. Cash directed his attention at his little man carrying 100 bandz in a duffle bag that he planned on blowing tonight.

"Take that bitch 5 bands," he said referring to the bartender. He didn't like the fact that she acted like he wasn't going to pay for the bottles. His little man pulled out the cash and walked off. Cash popped a bottle of Spades open and took a sip. His team knew the drill, and each of them grabbed a bottle of Spades and Ciroc before they turned up, gang banging hard and two-stepping to the music. Cash sat back and watched his niggas do them, as the DJ played all the latest hits. The champagne and kush smoke filled the air, and he felt like a boss. His boys didn't waste no time getting a few bad bitches to show them love. He was in his element – he lived for the bright lights and all eyes on him. He made it his business to shine bright like a diamond. They looked like money, that's what life was about, shining on these niggas.

"Ah Killa, go pay the DJ to play Cash Moody song "The Team" for me one time. Tell Mook to get us 50 Gs in ones. We bout to make it rain real quick," he said, taking a sip from his drink and hitting one of the blunts that was in rotation. June came over and sat next to him, clinging to a bottle.

"How you feeling, Skud?" he yelled over the music

"Like I run the world," Cash said, feeling himself. He put his drink on the table and threw his arm around June's neck.

"Look at us, my nigga," Cash said, pointing at his team. "We having our way on these streets, niggas respect us everywhere we go B. The guys ain't done it this big since Marvell in the 90s, my nigga. We a fucking movement," he added before leaning back in his seat.

"Yo ass crazy Skud, no lie," June said, shaking up with him. "Where the fuck Mook at with my bag, my nigga? I need that drink, you try'na pour up?" Cash asked June.

"You already know," June replied, leaning back next to him.

"Y'all my niggas, no lie," Cash said, obviously drunk. Mook and Killa came back holding racks of ones.

"Pass that shit out before they play my shit," Cash stood up and yelled as a stripper came over to their table.

"You don't get nothing like this nowhere, everybody move like brothers. And everybody from different places, Milwaukee, St. Louis, Detroit. You know what I'm saying? We got people from everywhere in our mob. Everybody moves as one, everybody posturing in some kind of way. Every man plays his role, and everything starts with the leader." Big Meech came in on the chorus talking big money shit, and they begin to make it rain. Cash grabbed the stripper pulling her onto his lap. She began to dance on him. He watched money fall all over them. Moody's song "The Team" wasn't a club hit, but he rapped about the life Cash was living. The stripper turned around facing him. She was hands down the baddest bitch in the club. Her hazel eyes were magnificent.

She whispered in his ear, "Where Angel at?" She asked pushing against him feeling his hard dick.

"Over there," he pointed in their direction. Kia's mouth fell open when she saw Angel and Money sitting at another table. She stood up and backed away.

"I'm so sorry, I thought you was somebody else," she said, turning to walk away. He grabbed her arm.

"Where you going, Ma? The real money right here," he yelled so she could hear him. Kia let out a long sigh, slowly spun around, and looked him up and down. He was sexy like his twin, but she wanted the certified thing not some look alike.

"I'm good, baby," she said, yanking her arm free and walking away. Cash looked back at Money's table. He knew Angel delivered his message because Money didn't look happy to see him. So he went to mess with him a little bit.

(MONEY)

Money saw Cash and five of his niggas headed and his direction. When they reached the table, Cash just smiled.

"What's good, Money? I see your broke ass made it home." Money shook his head.

"I see you think you Kevin Heart try'na be funny and shit. I ain't been broke in over 15 years," Money smirked.

"So you got that lil money I gave Angel to help you get on your feet. I wasn't gone give you shit. But then what type of kingpin would I be, having my bro running around fucked up. I just came over so you could thank me and wish you the best with this little club," Cash said, trying to sound convincing. "What you make 100 Gs a month? That's cool, but I get that every other day," Cash stated. Money stood up and walked around the table to get at Cash, but one of his hitters stepped up. Money hit him with a left hook putting him on his ass. Just as fast as he buckled, he was right back up clenching a .40, which he put to Money's forehead, but before he could pull the trigger, Cash stepped between them. The bouncers ran over to break up what was left of the brawl. June attempted to get at Money but he realize it was impossible. So he stood his ground with a smirk on his face.

"Imma see you boy," he said as he pointed his finger like a pistol and pulled the trigger, indicating he was gone kill him. He didn't play games and was with the shits when it came to gunplay.

"Calm down, we don't want no trouble," Cash said, putting his hands in the air with a grin on his face. The bouncers escorted them outta the club. Cash made it rain throwing bandz in the air as they left. Money couldn't believe his brother came at him with them young dummies. Angel walked over to him.

"It's ok baby, we gone show him. You the boss nigga," she said. He loved how she always had his back.

"Yeah I know." Twenty minutes later, the party was over and the club emptied. After closing the club, Angel and Money went home and went to sleep.

Chapter 4

MONEY,
9:00 A.M.

oney got up after a good night's rest. He made his mind up. He didn't need Cash to get paper. A lot of niggas talked that big money shit, but he got off on running the streets. He didn't require Cash to get to them bandz, he moved work on his own. He'd be lying if he said he wasn't looking forward to being a millionaire off the bandz he gave Cash. Today he was getting back in the game. He was going to Madison to do his thing. It was time to take the city back, he just needed to put a team together. It was relevant to show Cash who was the broke nigga. That stunt he pulled gave him all the motivation he needed. He was working with $250,000 as start up money, it wouldn't get any better than that. He wouldn't have a problem turning up. At one point in his life, he got it out the mud. Coming up from shit with nothing but $80 and an 8 ball, so being able to afford a brick and still have the hunger of a broke nigga was a deadly combination. The streets better watch out, the king was back and fully motivated.

(ANGEL)

Angel was in the shower getting ready for work . She'd talked with Kia about everything that happened last night. She knew Money was getting back in the game after that show Cash put on last night. His pride wouldn't let that go, and being the kind of woman she was, she had his back. She would never forget the day they arrested her man and all his niggas ratted him out. Angel wanted him to have loyalty on his side. Today she planned to confess about her and Kia, and pray for him to be understanding and put Kia on his team. Kia was a ride or die bitch and that's what he needed in order to stay out.

"Can I come in?" Money asked, but didn't wait for an answer. He opened the shower and stepped in behind her. She turned around and stared into his eyes, wrapping her arms around his neck, and kissed him passionately. His lips were so soft that she lost herself in them. She felt his dick harden as the hot water ran down her back. He pushed her against the wall lifting one of her legs up and entering her. Angel let out a loud moan and grabbed a handful of his locks.

"I love you," he whispered in her ear before kissing her. She loved the way his hard chest presses against her breast. Her nipples were hard and she began to cum as he picked up his pace, fucking her so good that she felt she might suffocate. The dick was so proper it was taking her breath away. She glanced into his eyes as she came. Angel cherished everything about him. She didn't have one complaint. He continued to stroke, slowing it down to make love. She took his chocolate face and kissed it.

"Let me suck it," she whined. He placed her down and then she dropped to her knees sucking him as the water ran down her face. Just seeing the expression on his face as he endured the warmth of her mouth turned her on even more. He was flawless, God's gift to her. She used her hands to jag his dick off using a twisting motion, then deep throated, swallowing his entire dick.

"I'm nutting, Ma." She stroked his dick letting his nut squirt down her throat. After swallowing every drop, Angel stood up. He removed her wet hair from her beautiful face, and she took a towel and began to wash him up. He was her king, and she treasured their connection, conversations, and his company. She would do anything to keep him safe.

"I'm getting back in the game," he said, gazing in her eyes. He saw the pain in them, and he hated hurting her or seeing her suffer.

"I knew already," she replied, understanding there was nothing she could do to change his mind. She stepped out the shower, taking a towel from the shelf to dry off.

"When you done, meet me downstairs so we can talk," Angel said, leaving the bathroom. Once in their room, she picked up her cell phone and dialed Kia's number.

"Hey Boo," Kia said happily when she picked up.

"Girl, come to the house, we need to talk," Angel said as she begin to lotion her body sitting on the bed.

"Isn't Money there?" Kia asked uncertainly.

"Yeah, I'm about to tell him about us," Angel said nervously.

"About time, Bitch," Kia screamed excitedly.

"Girl, you crazy. He ain't been home but a day, you must really want to see what that dick do," Angel laughed, putting the phone on speaker as she put on her thong and bra from Victoria Secret.

"You already know this, and I think this was your plan all along. To have us both," Kia stated.

"Girl, just get over here you, might get what you looking for," Angel said.

"Well, I'm on my way." Angel hung up the phone just as Money walked out wrapped in a towel.

"What we need to talk about?" he asked, walking over and sitting next to her on the bed. Angel stood up to get dressed.

"So what's your plan this time?" she asked, getting down to business.

"Angel, the streets don't change, just the players. Don't worry about this type of shit. I told you before, the game ain't up for discussion," he announced firmly. He despised talking business with her. He felt the less she knew, the better. That way, if he went down, they couldn't put her in the middle of his shit. He trusted her but still believed a person couldn't tell what they don't know. She wasn't a street individual and she didn't have the cold heart it took to run the streets. That alone was a weakness and he wasn't willing to chance it.

"What if I could help?" she asked, stopping what she was doing to come over and stand in front of him. She put her hands on her hips and her legs began to shake from the nerves taking over her body. She prayed this was the right decision because she couldn't live with out him. He was her rock when she was weak, and he never took advantage of her heart. She couldn't keep lying to him, she had to be honest.

"Help me how?" he questioned, confused.

"First, there's something I need to confess," she said as tears rolled down her face. She dipped down to her knees to stare in his eyes.

"Why are you crying?" he asked, wiping away her tears.

"I'm sorry Baby. I cheated on you," she whispered as tears flowed down her face.

"What?" he said, surprised, jumping off the bed. She saw frustration and pain in his eyes.

"Bitch, you cheated on me?" he asked with deep rage and narrow eyes.

"Yes, with a woman," she cried. A feeling of relief washed over him because in his mind that wasn't cheating since she slept with a woman. What real man would be angry with that? When she said she cheated, he automatically thought it was a man. He was committed to her and wanted the same in return. He couldn't imagine another man in between her thighs, but a women was different. It was his dream to have a threesome.

"Don't worry about that, Ma. I forgive you. But how could this help?" he asked, giving her a hug to show her confirmation that everything was ok.

"She can help you get back in the game. A lot has changed out here since you been gone, Baby, and I don't wanna see you get locked up." She told him all about Kia and how she knew what she was doing. Angel informed him about Kia's team, and how loyal she was. Money took time to ponder the information Angel was throwing at him.

"That could work," he said.

"It will work," she stated. "The police got you the last time because they knew what to look for, but this time they wouldn't with a team of bitches."

"What you know about trapping?" he asked, joking around with her and wiping the remaining tears from her face.

"Everything. I learned from the best," she replied with a smile.

"When Imma meet her?" he asked anxiously.

"She's on her way over now," Angel revealed proudly.

(KIA)

Kia knocked on Angel's door. When Money opened it, she saw him up close for the first time. He was finer than she previously remembered. His dreads hung down to the towel wrapped around his waist. His chest was big and full of muscle. She couldn't help thinking he had the best body she ever laid eyes on.

"Is Angel home?" she asked, unaware if Angel already confessed.

"Come in," he said, looking her over. She was sexy as hell, he thought, and his dick jumped in the towel. He imagine how she looked naked and it began to harden. She looked down and smiled. She knew he liked Angel's taste from the way he was staring. She was thick in all the right places. She walked in with her swag turned up and he peeked at her ass. It's been years since she received some dick, but he turned her on. She would give him some pussy in a split second. He was fine, but a little too sexy for her. Men like him broke hearts, and she wasn't try'na get hurt. Her heart couldn't take it.

"So where is Angel?" Kia asked.

"She's in the living room. You know where it's at?" he asked, knowing she did. Kia didn't respond, she just made her way to the living room. Angel was sitting on the couch. Kia walked over and Money followed her.

"Is everything ok?" she asked.

"I told him about us," Angel stated, coming right out with it. Kia glanced over at Money. His expression showed he was enjoying the situation.

"He's ok with it?" she asked seductively.

"Yeah Bitch, but right now you're here for something else."

"Like what?" she asked with a skrew face.

"Business," Money said.

"What business do we have other than a threesome?" she responded, rolling her neck.

"Girl, you crazy!" Angel laughed. "Money, this is Kia, and Kia, this is my man," Angel said, introducing them.

"Nice to meet you in person. I've heard a lot about you," Kia said, staring at his towel licking her lips.

"Nice to meet you, but let's get down to business. We should have time for all that freaky shit later," he said.

"I hope so, but what business do we have?" Kia asked.

Angel jumped in. "Girl, I told you about Money and what he was arrested for. I hoped he would've changed being locked up five years, but he didn't. He's getting back in the game, and I want the right people behind him." The words "behind him" pissed Kia off. She wasn't a worker, the only kind of work she did with a boss was legit. When she hustled, she was her own boss.

"What you mean, like work for him? Because I don't do that," Kia said, getting offended. She stood up to leave. Angel reminded Kia of her past, and she didn't have time for this shit. Money saw his chance slipping away, and he didn't want to miss out on this opportunity. The more he thought about Angel's idea, the better it sounded to him. He needed to make this thing work.

"Look, I know you don't know me, but I don't fuck around. Give me a year, and I'll make you rich. We gone be partners, every dollar we make we split 50/50," he said. Kia was speechless. It was a lot to take in. She thought she was coming over to have sex not talk business. She was a businesswoman and hustling with someone like him was a big deal, but getting the chance to be his partner was a once in a lifetime opportunity. When Angel told her about him, she googled him and found out the feds wanted his case. But they weren't confident in the state's investigation and chose not to pick it up. They estimated he was worth millions in drug money. She thought about it and couldn't let this opportunity pass her up. He made all the right points. She was a boss and didn't work for anyone.

"Ok, I'm in, but what we moving?" she asked.

"Cocaine," he replied nonchalantly.

"Nah, that ain't where the money at. Heroin where the real cash at," she said, taking a seat again.

"Heroin, I don't have a connect for that," he commented out loud but really to himself.

"I know this African, he's big in the heroin business, Imma talk to him," Kia said.

"When you gone do that?" Money asked.

"Imma get on it right away," she said. "then we going to Madison. I got us a spot set up already through an old friend. I'm meeting him in the morning. You think you'll have everything set up in two days?"

Kia thought about it. She understood the sacrifice needed to be made in order for the supplier to do business with her. She didn't wanna deal with the extra shit, but something was telling her this was a chance of a lifetime deal.

"Yeah, I'm going to get on it now," she said, standing and kissing Angel on the lips.

"Thanks," Angel said, giving her a hug. Money saw her out. When they made it to the door, she turned and faced him.

"Too bad I don't mix business with pleasure," she flirted, opening his towel and grabbing his fat dick, "because I bet this would've been fun," she continued before walking out the door, leaving him standing there. Kia got inside her 2010 Infiniti feeling amazing. She started the car and pulled off. A lot was running through her mind about the deal with Money. It could potentially change her life. She was determined to do whatever was necessary to make adjustments with her life. She was optimistic about her future, the only thing it required was for her to bargain with the devil.

(MONEY, 2:00 P.M., MADISON)

Money pulled up to his old friend's house in an all black rented Camaro. He wasn't in the Bentley; Madison was too small for such a flamboyant car. He road through his old hood, Allied Drive, and shit looked excellent. They were cleaning up the hood and it was unacceptable for business. There was no life when he was running the block, fiends were everywhere try'na hustle to get high. He got out the car and walked to one-eyed Larry's apartment building. When he made it inside the building, it looked spic and span. It pissed him off. They really was trying to purity the slums, but that was gone change. He knocked on the door, and Larry opened it with a big smile on his face.

"A-Money! What it do?" he said, trying to be cool.

"Same shit, try'na take over the world."

"Then come in," he said. Inside Larry's house was nice and clean. If he didn't know better, he would've thought a woman lived there. But Larry's wife passed away six years ago from an overdose. When she passed, it devastated everyone from the hood. She was the hood's big mama, always telling them what to do. Even though she was a fiend, everybody respected her.

"What you got plan, Nephew?" Larry asked, rubbing his glass eye.

"I'm looking to open up shop," Money said, taking a seat in the living room.

"Talk to me Nephew. Tell me something good," Larry said, rubbing his hands together.

"What you know about heroin?" Money asked.

"The question should be, what I don't know, cuz that's my first love."

"Tell me something good then," Money asked, sitting back in his seat.

(MEANWHILE)

Kia called Danjunema to inform him she needed to see him. He was more than delighted to meet with her. She resented having to travel to Chicago to meet him downtown at his office. She hated driving outta town in the winter, the snow scared her. The ice that formed on the roads could end yo life in a second, but she couldn't miss the meeting with the man that could change her life. He wasn't just a drug lord, he was a businessman and a real important one at that. Before she entered the building, she was stopped by his security and patted down, then allowed to enter. They led her to his office and told her to have a seat in the waiting room while they went to get the boss. But she didn't listen and walked right in. Dajunema sat behind his desk.

"Nice to see you, Kia," he said, taking in her body. He would sacrifice anything to be with her one more night. In the past he even tried paying her, but she always turned him down.

"Hi," she said, giving him a hug.

"So, what can I help you with today? And let's make it quick. I have an appointment to get to," Danjunema said, picking up some papers off of his desk.

"Well, I'm here on business, and I'm in need of your help," she responded, taking a seat.

"What kind of business we talking about?" he asked, looking up at her smiling.

"Heroin. I'm looking for a supplier," she said nonchalantly.

"Oh…. I might be able to help you with that. How about we talk about this over dinner tonight?"

"That works," she said, a little annoyed and standing to leave. As she gave him a hug, this time he grabbed her ass and she didn't resist. She knew what he wanted and if he gave her the work for the right price, she was willing to fuck. It was her time to get paid, and she was going to work this in her favor the best way possible.

(CHICAGO)

It took Tre Boi, Big Ryan, and the rest of the team two hours to bag a brick of crack and a 100 grams of boy. Once they saw June was serious about hustling, they put the rest of their money up for the

100 grams. All the windows in the spot were boarded up and there were three 2x4 on each door. June wanted to make it tough for 12 to kick in the doors. He put Tre Boi and Ryan in charge of the hustling operation. Out of their guys, he knew they'd take them to the next level. He wouldn't have to worry about them being selfish. They were BD crazy. Outside more than 60 hypes where lined up for a pass out. They were about to give all the fiends a free bag of boy and girl, along with the number to call the spot before coming. Ryan took most of the work to the back and put it in a duffle bag. When he walked back up front, Tre Boi had already started passing out work. The hypes were pushing each other try'na get a bag. When he walked outside he yelled.

"Ay, chill the fuck out, everybody gone get a hit," he said with his .357 in his hand. The fighting stopped once they saw Ryan holding his gun. He walked back inside because it was cold as shit out there. It took 20 minutes to move the line and make sure everybody was able to test their product. They weren't worried about them coming back, that was a given. They turned the brick of coke into a brick of crack. Not one gram extra, to have the best product possible. With the fish scale, Cash could've easily turned one into too. When they told June the idea, he didn't understand it but told them to do them.

"Ay Ryan, ain't no more blunts," Tre Boi said, coming out the back. He was 5'9", dark skin with a short cut and a gold grill. Ryan was 5'10" with carmel skin, locks down to his back, and a little overweight.

"Hell naw, we smoked the last few."

"Damn," Tre Boi said, going in his pocket and pulling out $10. "Ay, Blue, hit the store and grab some blunts."

"Fuck I look like nigga?" Blue said, walking past him heading to the bathroom. Ryan took the money.

"I got it, that's the problem around here. Everybody wanna be tough," he said, putting on his hoodie and heading out the door.

"Shit," he yelled when the cold hit him. He didn't put his hoodie over his head, he wasn't try'na be lacking. He walked a block before he saw a blue Cadillac head his way. It was the same car at the scene when one of the homies got murdered. He pulled his .357 revolver from his hip and begin to backpeddle. He knew he didn't have enough shots to stand his ground, so he aimed with a two-hand grip and fired a shot. Bloc!

The round hit the front windshield. He hoped to back them off, but instead two masked man hopped out and returned fire.

Bloc! Bloc! Bloc! Bloc! Bloc! Bloc! Bloc!

He got low, used the cars as a shield, and took off running. He heard bullets smacking into cars and homes. The shooter gave chase, stopping from time to time to let off a shot. He turned left and a gangway stopped at the end. When one of the shooters turned the corner, he was hit with a burning force to the chest. Bloc! Bloc!

Ryan watched him fall before taking off again. The other shooter jumped over his body and continued chasing him. Bloc! Bloc! Bloc! Bloc!

Ryan could hear the bullets flying past his head. He prayed to God he didn't lose his life today, and God must have heard him because Blue bent the corner with an assault rifle. Ryan stepped to the right, getting out the way.

Brrroc! Boc Boc Brrroc!

The shooter stopped giving chase and returned fire before taking off running. Blue was about to run him down when they heard sirens. They took off and ran a half a block to the back door of the spot. Tre Boi let them in. Ryan was outta breath and dropped down on the floor.

"Get yo fat ass up," Tre Boi said laughing. Blue went up front to watch the security cameras. The police were everywhere. Ryan and Tre Boi came up front to the kitchen.

"What happened bro?" Blue asked.

"Man, as soon as I hit the corner, I saw the G-boys coming up the block," Ryan said outta breath.

"So you was right," Tre Boi said to Blue. When they heard the shots, Blue grabbed the AK and ran outside. He had told Tre Boi he thought the G-boys was on Ryan. The trap phone rang, and they all looked at it.

"I guess hustling over with for the day," Ryan said, thinking about the body up the street he just dropped. It would be a while before 12 left.

(LATER THAT NIGHT IN MILWAUKEE)

Money was at the crib after spending the day at Larry's house. He learned a lot about heroin or "boy" as Larry called it. Kia was right, it was the new cash cow. He found out grams sold for $100 in Madison to other hustlers and went for $250 to the hypes. Larry told Money a reasonable price to get work from a supplier was 70 dollars a gram. Larry told him that "Madison didn't have any solid dope and needed some raw." Whoever had the elite product would make the most currency hands down. Money prayed Kia would come through on her part because if everything was proper, they would be rich. Angel strolled in the room, coming over to Money rubbing his back.

"How things going, Daddy?" she asked, rubbing her fingers through his locks.

"Good on my end, Ma. Real good, I just hope yo girl come through."

"She will, Kia's someone you can depend on. Trust me," Angel assured him. Money grabbed his pre-rolled blunt and flamed it up. Angel told him to sit on the floor and began to braid his locks straight to the back. He took two pulls and let out a cloud of smoke.

"So Ma, tell me about yo girl," he asked, pulling from the blunt.

"What you wanna know, Baby?" she asked, putting oil on his locks.

"Tell me how y'all started fucking around."

"It just happened one night, when we was drinking," she lied. She couldn't tell him about the murder Kia committed. She promised to take it to the grave.

"I wanna know more, Ma, like how it felt to you," he said, putting the blunt out and taking a sip of his lean.

"You nasty, that's all," she replied, pushing his head playfully and he laughed.

"I'm for real though," he said.

"Ok Nasty. Well, it felt like I was in heaven. It was like every time she touched me, licked me, my body wanted more, needed more. The feeling of her breast against mines, her soft hands, it was amazing," she said as she exhaled and wrapped her legs around his body. Going down memory lane turned her on.

"Damn, that shit must've been good, cause it's hot as hell between your legs," he said and they broke into laughter.

"Nah, for real Baby, Kia a good person and very loyal," Angel said on behalf of her girl. Money sipped on his double cup and Angel finished braiding his hair. He got up and looked in the mirror making sure he was straight. Angel turned on some music playing "Still" by Tamia. As she began undressing, Tamia sang her heart out. "Still, feels like the first time we met, that we kissed and I told you I love you, we still run around like teenagers even though we grown and married with kids." Money spun around and Angel was laid on the king size bed playing with her vagina.

"Come put a baby in me, Daddy," she said. He smiled and walked over to tease her wet box.

"I'm gonna ride with him till the wire, our love is never gonna end we on fire," Tamia continued to sing as they made love.

(MEANWHILE – KIA)

Kia was downtown at the Ritz Carlton Hotel with her lips around the smallest dicks she ever laid eyes on. It's been a long time since she gave head, but something she'd never forget is how to drive a man crazy. She kissed the tip then slid her warm lips around his dick, taking it in her mouth. She sucked on him until his toes curled. He couldn't contain the euphoria building up inside him. When he was ready to nut she pulled his cock outta her mouth.

"70 dollars a gram? That's too much, Imma need you to go lower, how about 50?" she asked, licking her lips seductively putting her head down to give the tip another kiss. He was so turned on he'd do anything.

"Ok," he said, hoping she would shut up.

"One last thing, Imma need it fronted to me," she said, taking all of him into her mouth.

"Yeah, how about a key, will that work?" he asked as his eyes rolling to the back of his head.

"Yeah," she returned with sex appeal. Kia understood that sex was the best way to manipulate a weak man. He pushed her head down in his lap fucking her face until he nutted down her throat. She made sure she swallowed.

"All better?" she asked before getting up.

"Yeah, much better," he said.

"Let's get back to business, Imma need you to get it ready tonight," she said.

"Tonight don't work," he said, getting himself together. That was the best head he'd received in his life. "In the morning Imma have it dropped off at your house," he continued, pulling up his pants.

"You know where I live?" she asked, surprised.

"Kia, I don't do business unless I know everything about the person I'm working with. This is a big boy game and I don't play about my money. I hope you remember what transpired last time." She knew if she fucked up, she had two ways of payments. But you have to pay to play.

"Yeah," she said. "Ok then, let's do business."

Chapter 5

1:00 P.M.
THE NEXT DAY

When Money walked out the door, he felt the Wisconsin winter at its worst. It was snowing and the roads had black ice on them. But it was nothing to him, he learned a long time ago to navigate his way through the worst it could render. He jumped into his Bentley feeling like new money. Last night Angel got a text message from Kia saying things were a go, they would be leaving in two days. He was really feeling his all black Dolce and Gabbana jeans and shirt that Angel picked out for him to wear, but what set his attire off was his $600 Pierre Hardy high top shoes. He pulled off in trap mode today, and it reminded him of the old days when he used to hit the block at night dressed in all black, try'na make a come up. Only difference was the type of money he was chasing. Back then he was selling dimes, now he could sell bricks if he wanted. But that wasn't his style, he liked to break his shit down to see a bigger over all profit because many smaller sales led to bigger gains. If you stay down and grind for long enough, it would show. It felt pleasant to be in control of his life again. He was allowed to go anywhere he desired, no more C.O. telling him where he was allowed. He jumped on I90 heading to Beloit to meet Lo Lo, his guy he met in the joint. Lo wanted him to come through to pop a bottle. A hour later, he pulled up on Portland. Lo Lo was perched on top of his 2015 Lexus GS, smoking a blunt. Lo Lo was a tall light-skinned dude. They became friends in prison. In the joint, Madison and Beloit niggas rode together under the (608) coalition against Milwaukee and Racaine. Money parked the Bentley and stepped out.

"I see you Bro, you didn't waste no time did you," Lo asked, giving him a manly hug and passing him the loud.

"Ya, I had to fuck em up bro, after being down five years," Money said, looking across the street at a group of niggas watching them.

"We good out here, Bro," Lo said, noticing Money glance across the street at them. Lo knew he didn't bring a banger with him. "What, you think I'm lacking?" Lo said, showing his 40 with a 30 clip on his waist.

"Nah, I ain't saying that Bro, I'm just try'na stay on point, that's all my nigga," he said sitting on the car.

"Nigga, we can always go inside if you scared," Lo joked.

"Nigga, you got me fucked up," Money laughed.

"What's new, Bro?" Lo wondered, going into his car to grab a bottle of Hennessy.

"Shit man, same shit. Thinking of a plan."

"You one thinking muthafucker, no lie. What you try'na get into?" he asked before hitting the bottle and pulling his locks into a ponytail.

"I came to fuck with you," Money said, shrugging his shoulders.

"Then let's go inside, Bro, cuz it's cold as hell." Money followed him into his house. It was small, but laid the fuck out.

"Ah, Lo who is that?" the woman on the sofa asked as they walked through the door.

"Damn Bitch, relax," Lo said with a screw face. "Bro, have a seat. Imma go holla at my girl real quick. Oh ya, this Thotianna, I mean Re Re, my girl sister," he added before walking down the hall. Money sat beside her and flamed up another blunt.

"So what's your name," she asked.

"Money."

"No boy, your real name," she asked, turning to face him, batting her eyes.

"Money," he replied firmly.

"Whatever," she said, rolling her eyes as she got up and went to the back. He watched her ass jiggle and the little ass shorts she was wearing. She was cute but not his type. When she came back, she had changed into some even smaller shorts and flopped down next to him on the couch. He had to admit, she was thick and he wouldn't mind hitting that.

"Can I smoke with ya?" she asked, licking her bottom lip. He passed her the loud, and she took a big pull and began to cough.

"You aight, Lil Mama?" he asked, laughing.

"Ya, I'm cool," she said, still coughing, passing the blunt back. She went to get some water. This time when she got up, half her ass hung out. It was starting to turn him on. Her ass looked soft, like it made waves when fucked from the back. He was willing to bet she couldn't take dick. Most thick girls couldn't take big cocks. "You want something to drink?"

"Nah, I'm good" he responded softly.

"You don't talk much I see," she asked coming back with her water.

"You talk too much," he shot back.

"Sorry," she said rolling her eyes and sitting back down.

"Nah, I'm just fucking witchu," he said hitting the blunt. "Where the ash tray?" She stood up to get it. He got another view of her fat butt. Damn she thick, he thought. She came back and handed it to him and he ashed the tip of the blunt.

"Won't you go put on some clothes, Ma," he said passing her the loud.

"Boy, don't tell me what to wear, you ain't my man," she shot back. Money smiled.

"You got that, Ma."

"I know I do, cuz I ain't fucking you. And if I was, you still wouldn't tell me how to dress," she said shooting him the evil eye.

"So what you saying is I could fuck you?" he questioned.

"Boy ain't nobody say shit like that," she laughed.

"Stop playing, you know you feeling me," he shot back.

"You cute boy, but ain't nobody on that," she said, talking shit. "And anyway you wouldn't know what to do with me," she added.

"Where your room at?"

"What?" she asked, skrewing her face up.

"Where your room at?" he repeated, standing up putting his hands in his pockets.

"In the back, why?" she questioned.

"Cause I'm gone give you something to put in yo big ass mouth," he said, and her jaws fell open. She wanted to ignore him, but he didn't seem like the type of nigga to play games. She stood up and strolled down the hall to her room as Money followed her. He heard soft moans coming from the room down the hall.

"Boy, you better have a big dick," she said, walking in her room squatting on the bed. Money closed the door behind him and pulled out his 9-inch dick.

"You better know how to suck dick with ya big ass mouth," he said, but she didn't reply. She grabbed his dick lifting it up and begin sucking on his balls letting his dick rest on her face.

"Shit," Money said. She pulled his balls from her mouth and smiled before going back in for the kill.

(MEANWHILE: CASH)

Cash and the squad were at the tattoo shop. June was getting three 6-point stars on his chest to go along with the other 10 stars already there. These stars represented his body count. Cash stopped by to check on them and talk shit.

"Cash, tell me why your boy Mook let some niggas get down on him," Killa said try'na clown him.

"What happened B?" Cash asked, looking at Mook disappointed.

"Look, right, we on 85th and Songeman fucking with some hoes. When we came out the crib, a nigga on his way up the stairs. I guess this the nigga Bm crib right, so he look Mook in the face and asked Bro who he visiting. The nigga Mook lie talking bout he at the wrong crib, so I laughed, right. The pussy nigga ask me what's funny Bro," Killa said sitting down.

"So what you do?" Cash asked already knowing the answer. Killa pulled up his shirt showing his fresh ink on a 6-point star.

"Let's just say the nigga cost me 30 dollars." Everybody in the room broke out laughing except the tattoo artist who didn't understand the inside joke.

"Man, I'm outta here," Cash said, still laughing as he shook up with everybody. He pulled his hoodie over his head and headed out the door. He hopped in his 2016 Lincoln MKX and pulled off Jamming to Yo Gotti "DM." He drove up to Sharks, one of his businesses. They were selling wings out the front door, but you could buy the whole bird out the back if you was connected. He pulled in the lot and parked before calling T-Mack. He answered on the third ring.

"I'm outside," he said and then hung up. Three minutes later T-Mack came outside wearing an apron and holding a duffle bag. He got into the passenger side.

"What's good, Skud?" Cash asked as they shook up.

"Same shit B, that's 200 Gs right there," he said referring to the bag.

"Cool Bro, everything moving good?"

"Ya, it's still popping, Skud, but let me get outta here," T-Mack said and hopped out.

"Love," Cash yelled putting the bag in the back before pulling off. This was how he spent most of his days, picking up money. He rarely made drop offs. He wasn't trying to get caught with the work. He picked up his phone and called one of his lil thots. She answered on the second ring.

"What's good, Daddy?" she asked sounding sexy.

"You Ma, I'm try'na slide through," he said making a left and turned at the lights.

"You ain't gotta ask boy, just come." He smiled cause she was always ready when he called.

"Look though, I'm try'na do you and them three bitches that was over there last time," he said. She became silent for a second. "Ma, what's good, talk to me," he said, eyeing the road carefully. He needed to stay on point because of the war going on. She let out a sigh.

"You lucky I like you, boy. Imma see what I can do," she replied uncertainly.

"Hit me back when you know then," he hung up in her ear. When it came to women, he was standoffish and thought that a bitch was gone deal with him on his accord or not at all. Most females respected the game because he didn't sell them dreams. His iPhone vibrated in his lap, the screen read "little T.H.O.T."

"What's good?" he asked sounding annoyed.

"Come through in an hour. They'll be here," she said.

"Cool." He hung up the phone and turned the music up listening to Chief Keef "Flex" rapping, "I pull up, get my flex on, with a red bone, and her hair long."

(CHICAGO ON THE BLOCK)

The block had picked up today. Yesterday, the police stayed around try'na find information on the homicide that took place. It was Ryan's first body and he was on edge. He was a hustler, not a killer. Over the years he shot a few niggas in wartime, but a murder was different. He was a stand up dude and a trap star, so his mind was on the cash, and if or when the law came, he would hold court on the streets.

"What you want, Ti Ti?" he asked, try'na rush her out. She was telling him a long story he wasn't interested in. She ran her hand through her hair try'na fix herself up.

"Nephew, let me hold one till I get my check," she said. Ryan clutched her arm and led her to the door. He opened it and pushed her out. She yelled and told him not to put his muthafucking hands on her. He closed the door in her face.

"Bro, you know that's somebody OG, right?" Tre Boi asked, sitting on the table smoking a blunt.

"Ya, why?" Ryan asked.

"Cuz one of these days, a nigga gone lay you down for playing with they people," he said, passing Ryan the blunt. Big Ryan hit it and blew out the smoke.

"The last nigga that tried me in a coffin," he said, walking to the back where the rest of the guys were. The back room was full of smoke. They were playing 2k on the flat screen.

"Ay Blue, where June em at?" he asked taking a seat next to him.

"Bro, em went to get some tats earlier. They should be on they way back." Ryan pulled from the loud. He thought about June's plan and getting money. He wondered what they were gone do if Cash found out. He was confident June was thinking that far ahead.

"Ah Ryan, whatever happened to that little bitch Michelle?" Blue asked, breaking his train of thought.

"Oh that bitch ain't on shit," Ryan said waving his hind. Blue laughed.

"Nigga, you always say that shit when a bitch don't give you no pussy," he said clowning his mans. Ryan laughed. Blue was right. The bitch Michelle wouldn't let him fuck. So he stop fucking with the hoe.

"Nigga, at least I ain't like you waiting months to fuck shit! If a bitch ain't fucking, I'm gone. Point blank period," he said raising his voice a little. Blue smacked his lips.

"Ya whatever nigga, what happen with yo BM?" he asked, pausing the game to look at Ryan.

"Oh, that was different." Blue fell to the ground laughing and the whole room did as well. Ryan stood up shaking his head.

"Fuck ya'll niggas," he said slamming the door. Tre Boi was just letting a hype out the door.

"What it's looking like?" Ryan asked.

"21 hunnid," Tre Boi said putting the money in his pocket.

"That ain't bad for the first day," Ryan said putting his hand out to shake up.

"Hell naw," Tre Boi said shaking his hand. This was only the beginning.

(ANGEL: 3:00 P.M. IN MILWAUKEE)

Inside her bedroom Angel was cleaning up, she adored their beautiful estate. She worshiped the master bedroom, which overlooked the private, wooded yard. The bedroom was breathtaking with a tray ceiling, morning bar, refrigerator, and a built-in bookcase. She didn't have to leave if she didn't want to. She picked up her phone and called Kia, who answered laughing.

"What's funny?" Angel asked Kia, putting her on speakerphone and settling into bed, playing in her hair.

"Girl, you don't wanna know to keep it real, I'm thinking about going shopping or something," Kia said.

"Bitch, now you speaking my language," Angel said all hyped. Kia laughed knowing this bitch shopped until she dropped.

"I can't though, Angel. I gotta save the money I got," Kia said.

"Bitch, then why did you bring it up? Anyways don't worry about money, you good now you working with my baby."

"Oh yeah Hoe, why you didn't tell me he had a twin?" Kia asked smacking her lips.

"Cause he ain't on shit, bitch, that nigga a snake, point blank period." Angel said grabbing the remote control and changed the channel.

"Mmm hum, he gotta be to play his brother the way he did," Kia replied.

"I know right, had my baby looking all sad, I was ready to fuck him up," Angel said getting up to find something to wear. "So is we going shopping or what?" she asked.

"Yeah cause I need some new shit," Kia said sounding depressed.

"Who you try'na look good for, bitch? It bet not be for my man." Angel cocked her head back like Kia could see her.

"Bitch, I already told him, I don't mix business with pleasure."

"Yeah whatever. One of these days he gone fuck the shit outta us." Kia just laughed. Angel found her a pair of True Religion jeans and a hoodie with some Vault by Vans. She liked being comfortable while shopping. "See I know I'm right cause you didn't deny it," she added.

"Whatever, Bitch, just get ready. I'm on my way," Kia said.

"Love you," Angel said.

"Whatever," Kia said hanging up on her. *I'm gone kill that bitch,* Angel thought to herself before going to take a shower. Even though her and Kia were lovers, they were best friends as well. Kia was everything she required in a friend. Before Kia, she never had a tight friendship with a woman. Most females she met were imposters, and she always picked up on betrayal before it happened, ending their friendship. But with Kia, they just vibed from the beginning. Angel never hesitated when dealing with her. There was no envy, jealousy, or phony vibe coming from her. Angel turned off the shower and stepped out to get dressed. After drying off, she walked to her room naked and stopped to peek at herself in the mirror. Her body was flawless. She turned around to check out her ass then headed to get dressed. Twenty minutes later, she was ready to step out. Kia called telling her she was outside. Angel grabbed her clutch and headed out the door. When she made it to the car, Kia's appearance was sexy. Her hair was up in a bun. She was rocking an all red Chanel dress that fit her like a glove with some six-inch Jimmy Choo heels.

"Bitch, that's ya problem right there," Angel said pointing at her shoes.

"What?" Kia asked glancing down.

"Bitch, we going shopping, not out to the club, I ain't try'na hear you complaining while I'm shopping bitch." She was trying to shop for at least four hours. After two hours, Kia would be complaining with them heels on. "Imma get you another pair of shoes," Angel added opening the car door.

"Bitch, I brought my own."

"Oh," Angel said, closing the door sitting back in her seat. Kia starred at her friend. She really didn't play about shopping. For Angel it was a sport.

"Bitch, what you looking at? The mall only open until 9," Angel blurted out. Kia rolled her eyes and pulled off. Angel pulled out her iPhone and plugged it up to the AUX cord playing Usher "You Got It Bad."

"Oh hell no, Bitch, you know I don't do those love songs," Kia yelled turning the music down. Angel smacked her lips.

"Bitch, what you wanna listen to then?" Angel asked with a attitude.

"Girl, you can get mad all you want to. It ain't my fault Money got you in yo feelings," Kia said poking her in the face. Angel set there with her lips poked out looking like a big baby.

"I'm just playing, Girl, damn," Kia said, giving in to the sad puppy dogface. Angel didn't waste time pressing play, and Usher poured his heart out. "You got it bad, when you're out with someone, but you keep on thinking about somebody else." Angel danced in her seat mouthing the lyrics with last night's sex on her mind. They spent the rest of the day at the mall, buying everything they desired.

(AN HOUR LATER)

Cash was laid back getting his dick sucked by two bitches at the same time and watching the other two in a 69. He didn't know the girls' names giving him head. For the past 20 minutes, they took turns sucking him off. He came over with two-fifths of peach Ciroc and an ounce of loud. It didn't take much convincing to get them to have an orgy. The moment he walked through the door, they were all over him, and a thot bitch could smell money. He pulled his dick away from them.

"Who wanna be first riding this muthafucker?" he asked. They stared back and forth between each other, scared of the pain they would endure from it. His lil thot bitch Dria spoke up, lifting her head from eating the other girls pussy.

"Me, Daddy. These bitches acting like they never seen a fat dick before," she said, straddling him, fighting to put every inch inside of her. Dria was grunting and moaning louder and louder as she buried his pricker in her. Her friend watched amazed she could take dick so well. They couldn't believe she forced that gigantic cock all the way in her petite, tight pussy. She begin to shift up and down while one of the other females licked his balls taking them in her mouth one at a time. It wasn't long before the girl licking his balls wanted to sample the dick. She told Dria it was her turn. Dria got off his dick in straddled his face. The other two women were off to the side, one of them was getting her ass ate. The other bitch hopped on the dick and begin working his cock into her pussy, she was groaning and bucking. She was saying, "Yes, yes, fuck me Cash. Give me that big dick. Do it, baby, do it," acting like a complete slut, going crazy only taking half of it before she cum.

"Damn, bitch, yo pussy tight," Cash said pushing Dria off his face and putting his hands on the girl's waist, pulling her all the way down. She let out a loud moan as she came again.

"You like that, Bitch?" he asked. "Push down against me. You feel this big dick in there. Give me that pussy." She was too excited to last long and in a few minutes had a tremendous orgasm. He let her rest for a minute, then he continued to fuck the shit outta her. The Molly pill he popped had him feeling like Superman.

(LATER THAT NIGHT – MONEY)

Money made it home an hour ago. It was dark, he didn't know if it was the night or his emotions. He was feeling guilty from cheating on Angel. It weighed heavy on his heart. He couldn't face her right now, but he couldn't hide in his car forever, so he got out. He unlocked the house door debating on if he should confess, but quickly pushed the thought to the back of his mind. Angel was in the living room watching "First 48" when he came in.

"What you do today baby?" she asked, still looking at the TV. His guilt made him uneasy.

"Shit, why you ask?" Angel turned around with a mug on her face.

"What I can't ask my man what he been up to?" she questioned.

"Nah I ain't say that, I just thought you asked for a reason," he responded taking a seat next to her. She glared at him.

"Mmm hum, boy, don't get fucked up," she said looking at him suspiciously.

"What?" he asked scrunching up his forehead. She turned around and continued to watch T.V.

"Boy, you lucky I love you cause you acting like you been up to something."

"Whatever, Angel," he said standing up to take a shower.

While in the shower, a memory of Re Re sucking his dick flashed through his mind. He knew he would call her after the performance she put on.

"Nigga, I know damn well you ain't come straight home in get an the shower," Angel walked in the bathroom yelling. He opened the curtains.

"What?" he asked.

"Nigga, you heard me, I said I know you ain't bring yo ugly ass home and hop right in the shower," she repeated, rocking back in forth like a ghetto girl, her nostrils flared.

"Angel, gone somewhere with that bullshit, for real," Money said. She left slamming the door behind her. Money hopped out the shower ass naked without drying off. Angel was in the room on the bed. He grabbed her up and ripped off her boy shorts.

"Money, what the fuck," she tried to say but before she knew it, she was face down on the bed and he was eating her ass.

"Oh shit, Daddy, what's wrong with you," she moaned.

"Shut the fuck up, you think I was fucking, so Imma give you some dick," he said spreading her ass cheeks. He began to rub his cock across her pussy and entered her.

"Shit Daddy," she yelled. He got in the push up position, beating her pussy, changing the pace from fast to slow at the same time kissing her neck, back, and shoulders. She told him how sorry she was as she came over and over. They fucked for an hour until Angel had one more orgasm and then collapsed on him. After catching her breath, Angel sat up, still attached to Money, some of his dick still buried inside her. She rubbed his chest while slowly moving back and forth.

"I can't believe how good that felt," she said.

"It's been too long since I rode that dick," she continued.

"You just horny as always," Money said. She laughed.

"Horny for your big dick," she said and scooped up a handful of their combined juices from her cunt and tasted it. She finally rolled off him and they lay next to each other.

"You bet not be cheating on me, nigga," Angel said playfully. Little did she know, he'd just received the best head in the world and wasn't planning on ending the friendship.

(CHICAGO)

Damn, it's cold as hell, Blue thought as he made his way up the gangway with an AK47 in his hand. An hour ago he receive a call from one of his hoes about a dice game taking place in a house full of opps. Behind him two D-Boys were also holding assault rifles. Once they made it to the house, they split up. One of them went to the front and Blue and the other dude posted up on the side of the back door. They aimed at the door ready to snuff everything that came out.

Brrrroc! Brrroc! Brrroc!

Blue heard the shot come from up front as planned. He expected it to flush them out the back door. Just as he expected, the door flew open. An a crowd of six men came running out. The first one was holding a pistol in his left hand.

Blue aimed for him. Moc. Moc. Moc. Moc. The bullets hit him, spinning him around before he crashed to the pavement. The rest of them tried turning around but was shot down by his partner who took off running once he saw the bodies drop. But Blue took his time going through the dead man's pockets, relieving them of their cash and drugs. They wouldn't need it in the afterlife.

(THE NEXT DAY – KIA)

The city was nice and clean, she thought when she made it to Madison. Money said she was meeting him in the hood, but this block looked like the suburbs compared to Milwaukee slums. She met him using her GPS to get to Allied Drive. She had 100 grams of boy with her, that's all he wanted to start off with. She faked like she had to call for it but really had over a 1,000 grams at home. When he put the order in, she was disappointed. She thought he would've bought the whole thing. Kia was beginning to think she was in over her head. They gave Larry some of the work to try out 30 minutes ago.

"What the fuck is he doing back there?" Kia asked confused.

"Shit, I don't know," Money said, going to check on him. He knocked on the door. No answer, so he opened it. Larry was in the middle of a dope fiend node. Money laughed knowing the work was proper to put Larry on his ass. Larry came to.

"What's funny?" he asked.

"Shit, what's to it?" Money asked already knowing.

"I never had nothing this good," Larry said as Kia walked in.

"Then let's get to work. Kia Imma need yo help bagging this shit up," Money said. "We gone start right away, and Larry, I want you to set up a spot for the fiends to pick up their shit. I don't wanna meet nobody and I don't want nobody coming to this house. You get their cash, come here to get the work. Can you do that?" Money asked.

"No problem," Larry said, wiping the saliva off the side of his lip.

Money and Kia spent the next two hours bagging up and getting to know each other. It was easy to see why Angel liked her. She was a female version of him. He thought it was how sexy she was but she was more than just a pretty face. She knew a lot about the game, and she even put him up on shit he missed when he was locked down. He paid her $7,000 for the 100 grams. He was getting them for $70 a gram, so that was rational, or at least that's what Larry said. They would profit $18,000 off this deal. He was going to take the $7,000 back and let her keep the profit to show he was an authentic partner. Little did he know she was swindling him, selling him grams for $20 dollars more than she paid. She already made $2,000 off the 100 grams he purchased.

"Can I ask you something?" he asked, stopping from bagging up the work.

"Anything," she said with a smile. She didn't know him long, but he appeared to be a real nigga. He was outgoing, and she fathom it would be hard to stick to her rule of never mixing business with pleasure.

"What made a woman as fine as you stop fucking with niggas, or was you always into women?" Even though she didn't trust him yet, he made her comfortable enough to express herself.

"I used to fuck with niggas, but most of these niggas be lames, can't hang with a bad bitch like me. A lot of them want a bitch to bow down and let them run shit, but I'm a boss bitch," she tried to assure him.

"So you one of them females that wanna run her nigga, treating him like a bitch?"

Kia laughed, "It ain't even like that, I don't mind playing my role. But my nigga have to be a boss not some fuck nigga," she confessed.

"I understand that, but you ain't been with all niggas," Money said flirting with her. She didn't know what to say because she didn't want to betray Angel by messing with her man. They had discussions about a threesome, and Angel didn't have a problem with that, but she might if Kia fucked him alone without her present. Kia looked away.

"Boy, stop playing. The only way we doing something is if Angel around. As a matter of fact, I haven't talked to her today, how is she?" Kia asked.

"She fine. But we not talking about her right know," he said licking his lips seductively. He was beginning to turn her on. She need to battle the feeling and not let her pussy do the reasoning.

He walked over to her, leaned down, and said, "You gone be mines," kissing her neck. She let out a low moan. He was starting to drive her wild. Knowing how much she desired him gave him a deep surge of fulfillment. With his fingertip he gently caressed her neck and kissed it as well. He stroked her beautiful hair, barley touching her skin with his hands. She could have let him do this for hours but she had to get away from him. She stood up and walked around the table to do just that.

"We here for business and that's it," she said trying to sound convincing. He walked around the table and cornered her. Her eyes sparkled with lust and she saw the fire in his. She desired him with an intensity unlike anything she'd ever felt before. He kissed her and she closed her eyes and felt his chest press against her breasts. Their tongues tangled as he pressed his lips against hers. She opened her eyes and broke the kiss looking at the rest of his body, moving her hands along Money's neck, shoulders, arms, and chest. She couldn't get enough of his body and was overcome with lust. His hands wandered underneath the straps of her red negligee and slid it down her shoulders. He took off her shirt exposing her perfect round breasts. Kia nipples were hard and so was his dick as her hands began to roam over his body. Their breathing was heavy, their bodies hot. It was heaven for both of them. Just then, Larry entered the house moving fast and smiling hard.

"The word is out and I did some pass outs. I got somebody that want 10 right now," Larry said walking in on them.

"What?" Money asked. "You got a hype with $2,500?"

"Yeah nigga, it's a white boy, they always spend big." Money passed him the work and he rushed out just as fast as he came in. Kia put her shirt back on, thankful Larry interrupted them before she made a mistake.

"We about to get paid," she said shocked that their first sale was $2,500. If she didn't comprehend before, she understood now that she made the right decision.

"Money, I can't fuck with you, I'm try'na get paid," she said walking to the restroom to fix herself up. She ran some water over her face, because she was worked up. She looked in the mirror.

"Come on Bitch, pull it together," she told herself before walking out. Money was seated at the table smiling.

"That's my bad, Ma, I know you said it's just business between us," he said walking up on her again. He moved in to kiss her again, but she moved away.

"We can't do this," she said in a soft voice, thinking about the feeling of his warm lips against hers. There was lust in her eyes, but she was fighting with herself not to fuck him, so he left her alone.

"Ok Ma, let's get back to work," he commented. She was thankful because she might've fucked him if he kissed her again. She couldn't remember a time a man had this much power over her. Money was trouble, somebody who could turn her whole world upside down. Love wasn't in her plans, she was trying to get paid. Not murder a nigga for breaking her heart.

(MEANWHILE – DANJUNEMA)

Danjunema sat in his office downtown with his mind on Kia. He was an important man and could have any woman he desired, and most nights he had them two or three at a time. But no matter how powerful he was, he couldn't have Kia. She was an independent woman that didn't believe in a man taking care of her. She wanted her own and he respected that about her. He was self-made and understood what motivated her. There was nothing like having power but not all understood what it took to earn it. It was essential to be a determined worker and be willing to make difficult decisions. Kia demonstrated the other night she had what it took. He was an intelligent man, and he fathomed if he wasn't a necessity as her connect, she would've never sucked his dick. It was the second best night of his life. They would have more sexual relations if she wanted him to continue doing business with her. He'd waited years to discover a way back into her life, and now was a great time because she needed him and he planned on holding it over her head. As long as she required his product, he needed some pussy. Little did she know he was the master at using what he had to his advantage.

(LATER THAT NIGHT – MONEY)

At 2 in the morning, Money and Kia sat at Denny's on Gammon Road after a solid day at the trap.

"You said you gone set up shop in the morning, right?" she questioned.

"Ya Ma, I don't mine getting up to get this paper," he repeated for the third time tonight. He begged her to come out with him, but she wanted to go to the hotel and sleep. When they left the trap, shit was wild. The fiends kept coming, and Larry made runs all day. Larry said the fiends wanted as much work as they could get. They feared it wouldn't be there long. It was the best product Madison had seen in 20 years and everyone coped from them. Word spread about the new raw on Allied.

"Shit I ain't got no problem getting up for those bandz either, but I still need my beauty rest. A bitch don't wake up like this, I don't care what Bee and Jay talking about," she said. Money smirked, he really dug her swag.

"I understand that but…"

"Stop, boy, anything after but is bullshit," she said cutting him off and schooling him at the same time.

"Aight," he agreed without hesitation. She had game that he respected.

"So tell me how you started trapping. What made a women as fine as you want to run the streets and play a man's game?"

"This ain't no man's game, I don't know why niggas think that when there's pussy niggas playing and winning every day," she said heated. Money didn't have a reply for that because she was right.

The game was smarming with hoe niggas. But most of them were eating and getting the most money.

"This is a game of will and power, and I got just as much will as the next nigga. Plus I got what niggas don't, the power of this pussy," she continued on.

"Your ass crazy, but you still didn't answer my question," he said being nosy.

"Bandz, just like you," she replied vaguely. She wasn't ready to reveal her past, and he wasn't going to push her to express something she wasn't prepared to.

"Cool, money is your motivation, I'm feeling that," he said pulling out his cash and leaving a 100 dollar bill on the table. He stood up and put his hand out for Kia to take. She took his hand, allowing him to help her up, but once on her feet, she showed frustration.

"Thanks, but I can stand on my own two feet," she said angrily.

"Damn, I'm just try'na be a gentleman," he said caught off guard.

"I know what you're try'na do, Money. This is only business, so stop it."

"Ok Ma," he said turning to leave. The ride back was awkward. They didn't say a word to each other. He knew she felt some type of way about him saying the streets was a man game. He wanted to express that he didn't mean any harm asking that question, but he understood sometimes a person just needed space to get over shit. He just hoped things worked out and returned to normal. They pulled up to the Sheraton hotel on John Nolen, he cut down the music, and retrieved the key to the room, handing it to her.

"Room 215," he said in a disengaged tone. "Imma be here to get you in the morning or whenever you ready, just call," he added.

"Where you going at 3 in the morning ?" she questioned.

"I'm gone bend a few blocks until it's time to open up the spot," he answered in an irritated tone. Who was she to be questioning him when she wouldn't even tell him why she entered the game? He wasn't feeling that at all.

"See you in the AM," he said as she got out the car. He pulled off and rode around the city before stopping at B.P. on Allied to grab a blunt. His mind was on pursuing them bandz and getting back on top. He rolled up a blunt and called Re Re.

(MEANWHILE)

Re Re woke up to answer her ringing iPhone. "Hello?" she said half asleep. When she heard Money's voice, she woke all the way up. "What's wrong, why you calling this late?" she asked, sitting up in bed.

"Damn, that's how you answer yo phone for a real nigga?" he asked.

"My bad boy, I just never expected to hear from you," she said.

"What made you say that?" he asked.

"I don't know! I guess it had something to do with how fast you ran outta here after what we did," she said with a smile on her face.

"Nah Ma, I just had something to do. It ain't have shit to do with you," he said.

"Ok, I guess."

"Ay, Re Re, tell me something about you," he said.

"Like what, Boy?" she asked, getting out of bed and getting her half a blunt she had put out before going to sleep.

"I don't know, anything, I guess, cause I'm try'na get to know you," he said. She couldn't hide the smile on her face if she wanted to. Ever since she laid eyes on him, he was all she thought about.

"Well, my name is Ashlee, but everybody call me Re Re. I was born in Chicago, but moved to Beloit when I was six months. My mom and dad were murdered when I was 11 years old. My sister raised me and took care of me since she was 20 years old," she said as a tear escape her eyes. It always hurt when she thought about her parents. The day they were murdered, her life changed for the worst. Her sister did her best, but Re Re rebelled against everything she said. When she turned 14, she started using her body to get what she wanted.

"I'm sorry to hear about your parents," Money said.

"It's ok, it happened a long time ago," she said, wiping the tears from her face.

"So how old are you?" he asked.

"I'm 19," Re Re said lighting up her blunt.

"Damn, you young, Ma."

"Whatever Boy, age ain't nothing but a number," she replied.

"You right about that."

"I know I'm right cause I suck dick like I'm 100 years old," she joked. Money laughed cause she wasn't lying.

"So tell me something about you," she asked, laying back on the bed wanting to get to know his fine ass.

(MEANWHILE – KIA)

Kia laid in bed thinking about Money. She was wrong for acting crazy with him tonight, but she had rules she needed to follow in order for him to respect her as his partner. She feen him and wanted more than just a friendship but it wasn't good for business. If they started having sex, she might fall in love with him. But what if he wasn't the right man and all they did was fuck, would he still respect her enough to be partners? She wished they would've asked her about hustling after they all had sex. She could still see his fat dick now, and before she knew it, her hands slid down her body. She found her clit and began to play with it, imagining the stories Angel told her about their amazing sex. Her nipples got nice in firm. She spread her legs wider as she began running her fingers all around the inside of her thighs and over her pussy. She was getting quite aroused, and soon her pussy was drenched from all the stimulation. She thought about how cut his body was and moaned, wishing her hands were his. She bit down on her lip, rotating her fingers across her clit before sliding two inside herself. She let out a muffled moan an felt the excitement building inside her, her body tingled all over as her finger moved with passion faster and faster as she had an orgasm. She thought about saying fuck the rules and giving him some pussy before she fell asleep.

(SUNDAY 5:00 PM)

When Kia woke up, she heard the shower running. She looked at her iPhone and it was 5:00 p.m. She had slept the whole day away comfortably in the lavish hotel room. She didn't feel like waking up but work needed to be done. She stretched her body and rose from bed. She heard the shower turn off.

"Money, is that you?" she asked knocking on the door. She pushed it open when he didn't answer. He stood there naked as the day he was born. Kia closed the door.

"Sorry, I didn't mean to walk in on you, I just wanted to make sure it was you in there," she thought about how dumb she sounded, who else would it be?

"Don't worry, it ain't like you never saw it before," he said referring to the day at the house. He walked out of the bathroom wearing nothing, and she had to admire his body. He looked like a Greek god. He advanced on her, stroking his dick. She stared as her pussy began to get moist from the erotic aspects of his body.

"Money, stop we can't do this," she said. They couldn't take it there because she wouldn't allow herself to.

"You know this what you want," he whispered as he brought his face towards her. Kia pulled away, but he drew her back taking control of her body. The way he glanced at her caused her to blush. He stared at her so intensely, she looked away.

"I do want it, but it's wrong," she whispered touching his face. She felt his hard dick on her thigh. She craved the passion it could bring. Before she knew what happened, he kissed her slowly and gently sucked her bottom lip and placed her hand on his chest. Her heart raced as she returned his kiss passionately. She took his dick in her hand and stroked it. It was so big, all she wanted to do was feel it inside of her, but she couldn't. This was so inappropriate. She pushed away before she did something she would regret.

"I can't," she said backing up into the bathroom and closing the door behind her. Her breath was caught in her throat. Damn, she really wanted him bad. Last night she said fuck her rules, she was gone fuck him, but not without Angel. No matter how much she wanted him, her heart belonged to Angel, and she was loyal to her. She turned on the shower and stepped in to cool herself down.

(AN HOUR LATER – KIA)

When she stepped out the bathroom, her mind was back on business. Money stood fully dressed looking handsome in Trues and a white T that fit him just right. She loved his swag, he wore his shit the correct way, never overdoing it. He was on the phone talking to somebody, and when she walked in, he hung up.

"Was that Angel?" she asked being nosy.

"Do I ask who calling you?" he questioned.

"No you don't, I was asking cause I missed my bitch, that's all," she mumbled, embarrassed.

"What you getting into?" he asked putting his phone in his pocket.

"Nothing. I don't know nobody up here, so what can I get into?" she said sarcastically.

"Then Imma need you to ride with me in a little bit."

"Where we going?"

"I gotta meet some niggas down here so they know I'm back in town."

"Ok that's cool, I can do that, but you need to rest. You been up all night."

"I'm good, Ma. First you ask me who calling me, now you telling me I need some sleep. Shit, you sound like my bitch," he said with a smirk.

"Boy, stop it, I just want to make sure you on point that's all. I'm just doing what Angel asked me to do, keeping you out of jail and making some cash as well," she said with a skrew face.

"Ya whatever, you starting to like the kid that's all," he said.

"Whatever, Boy, you ready?"

"Ya," Money said following Kia out the door. For the next three hours she rode shotgun with him. He linked up with all types of niggas and even some white boys that looked like drug money. He hadn't been to sleep in 24 hours and seemed ready to pass out at any moment, but was fueled by his love of money. She loved his dedication and the fact that he was motivated to trap like this, but he needed some rest and he wasn't gone listen to her.

So she texted Angel: *Call yo man and tell him to lay his ass down, the money gone be there in the morning.* After sending the text, his iPhone rang.

"Hey Ma, what's good?" he answered, talking to his wifey. "Alright," he said in agreement to what Angel instructed. "I love you," he said before hanging up.

"On what, you called my girl and told her I needed some rest?" he asked smiling.

"I didn't call her, I texted," she said, refusing to look at him.

"Somebody starting to like me," he joked.

"Ok whatever, Money, yo ass is crazy, I know that much," she said. He was an easy individual to like and such a short amount of time she started to care for him. When they made it back to the room, Money went straight to sleep. Kia went to the front office and checked into her own room. She didn't want to take the chance of fucking him, not that night at least. Once she made it to her room, she called her girl Ne-Ne informing her everything was fine and when the chance came, she'd put them on. She loved her, they'd been friends from day one. Her, Ne-Ne, and Tay Tay grew up together. They were the only consistent and unconditional love Kia ever knew other than Angel. Her entire world used to revolve around them. She loved her girls more than anything in this world, and they were all each other had growing up. She felt guilty working with Money without her team, but as soon as there was an opening, she'd get them in. Kia was a product of the ghetto, she grew up in Milwaukee on 9th and Keef and was born to a welfare mother who had nothing. They banked on government checks that came every first of the month. At a young age, Kia understood a 9 to 5 wouldn't cut it, so she learned how to hustle. She loved her mom, but couldn't depend on her, so she got it how she lived. She used to boost clothes with her friends. Even though it was a petty hustle, anything was game as long as it kept money in their pockets. She remembered the day she decided to enter the game.

They were 16 when they met him. He was an older man in his late 30s. At the time he owned a store they would boost at. One day her and her girls were in the store doing their usual thing. When he came from the back, he looked at her and said, "You come here." She thought about making a run for it, but that plan went out the window when two big dudes stood in front of the door cutting off the exit. She was the leader, so Ne-Ne and Tay looked to her for instructions, but she had no idea what to do next.

"I said come here," he pointed at her again. She walked his way with her head down. She knew he was going to turn them over to the police. She didn't want to go to jail, so she was thinking fast.

"You think it's ok to come in here and take my shit?" he yelled.

"No, I just…" she started.

"You just what? Think this shit free?" he said, cutting her off. "I've watched you little bitches come in here and take shit for months," he stated.

"But…"

"Anything after but is bullshit," he said cutting her of again. "Why are you stealing? And I want the truth," he asked. She looked in his eyes and thought about lying but changed her mind when she saw the coldness in them.

"Money," she said.

"What about money?" he asked.

"We take the clothes and sell them for money," she said putting her head down in shame. She understood it was wrong, but it was how they ate.

"If it's money you need, there's other ways to getting it. You are a cute little girl and could have anything you desire with hard work."

"You mean like work a job and make $8.00 an hour? That may be for some but it's not for me. I'm gone be rich one day," she promised.

"What you're looking for is a hustle, and this all you came up with?" he laughed in her face making her furious.

"What's your hustle, working out this store for the rest of your life?" she asked, rolling her eyes as if she made a point.

"No it isn't but Imma give you two choices. One is to go to jail, or two is to work here to pay off what you and your friends owe me. The choice is yours, so which one?" he asked.

"I'm not going to jail, that goes without saying, so I guess I'll work here," she said.

"Then I'm gone see you first thing in the morning. You can go now," he said, waving her off. For the next six months she worked eight hours a day without pay. Until she had enough. She went in his office and told him she was done.

"I quit," she said.

"I been waiting two months to hear you say that."

"What?" she asked, confused. She didn't comprehend what he was talking about.

"Your work here was done two months ago. I was just waiting for you to quit so I could show you a real hustle. Now that I know you're a person of your word," he explained.

"And what's that?" she asked, her mind wondering.

"The drug business," he said, standing up and pulling out a pound of kush laying it on the table. "This isn't much, but up here you can sell it for $4,000. Imma give it to you for $2,000, and you can profit $2,000 off each one," he said giving her the game. "I'mma set you up with a trap to sell it out of and the customers to sell it to. How does that sound?"

"So all I gotta do is sit back and wait for the people to come, and that's it?"

"That and make sure no one takes my shit cuz if they do, it's on you. See this is a man's game. I see you have the will and you're a hard worker, so I'm willing to give you a chance."

"I can do that," she said with a smile.

"Ok, we have a deal," he said.

Over the next year things went well for her and her team, they came all the way up. They had Smoke working the door, making sure no one robbed them. Smoke was a local killer, and everyone respected him. Everything was going smooth until Smoke robbed them blind one day taking 20 pounds. He said before leaving, "You bitches shouldn't be playing a man's game." Kia went home that night and cried. She didn't know what to tell the connect. The next morning she went down to the store to confess what happened.

"I told you this was a man's game, and now you have to pay the consequences," he said in a cruel voice that made her afraid. "You have two options. One, you can give me some pussy, or two, you can die. She didn't want to die that day, so she lost her virginity. That was the last time she took product from him on consignment until now.

Tears escaped her eyes as she reflected on her past. Smoke was her first body because he put fear in her heart she never felt before. It was her responsibility to make niggas respect her, and that day she turned cold towards men. She didn't show no love and her feelings were in check until now. Money was going to have her breaking plenty of her codes before it was all said and done.

(MONEY – TWO DAYS LATER)

"Imma need six grams," Larry said walking through the door. Kia pulled out the bag with over 30 grams and passed him the work. Money sat next to her playing 2k on the 72 inch flat screen TV he bought for the house. Since they were spending a lot of time there, he wanted to be comfortable. He took a pull from his blunt as Larry rushed out the door.

"This shit is crazy out here," Kia said referring to the traffic.

"Ya, this shit a gold mine," Money said putting out his blunt before pausing the game. He went to take a piss. While in the restroom, he heard the house door open. He washed his hands and headed back up front.

"Who was that?" he asked Kia. "Larry, somebody wanted 10 grams," she replied, sitting back down counting the money she received. Her phone lit up on the table and she picked it up.

"Hey, Girl," she said putting the phone on speaker and continued counting the money.

"Hey, Bitch, what y'all doing?" Angel asked.

"The same shit, in this house," Kia said putting a rubber band around the stack of cash.

"Where my baby at?" Angel asked.

"Right here playing this game," Kia looked at him sideways. "He heard you," Kia added.

"What's good, Ma?" Money yelled, keeping his eyes on the game.

"Hey, Daddy," she responded. Larry entered the house and ran straight to the bathroom.

"You good, Larry?" Money asked, jumping off the sofa nervously.

"Ya Boy. I gotta shit, that's all," he answered, closing the bathroom door behind him. They erupted in laughter.

"What's funny?" Angel asked being nosy.

"Shit, Bitch, you gotta be here to understand what's funny," Kia said laughing again.

"Well, I was just calling to check up on y'all," Angel said dryly.

"We good, Ma. I love you," Money said.

"I love ya'll too," Angel said, hanging up the phone.

Larry came out of the bathroom looking relieved.

"Damn, Larry, close that door!" Kia said grabbing her nose.

"My bad, Baby Girl," he replied and shut the door. "Imma be in my room for a little bit," Larry informed them. He needed to get high in order to keep moving this fast. The dope he took this morning was catching up to him, and he needed some rocks to stay awake.

Money put the controller down after losing with the Bucks to the Bulls. "I'm going to the store. You need anything?" he asked Kia. She shook her head no to busy on Facebook. He put his hoodie on before leaving, running to the Camaro to get out the cold. He started the car and picked his phone up to call Re Re.

"Hello," she said sounding all sexy. Ever since she sucked his dick, they've been texting and calling each other. She was down to earth and cool as hell, and he enjoyed her conversation.

"What's good, Ma?" he asked smiling hard before pulling off.

"That dick. When you gone let me suck it again?" she ask laughing. He made a left turn out of the lot.

"Imma send for you in a week," he said, grabbing his dick thinking about the good head he received.

"A whole week? That's too long, I'm coming tonight," she stated.

"Damn, Ma, you ain't playing," he laughed, turning on Carling.

"Nah I'm not. So what's up?" she asked.

"Ya, that's cool, just call me when you get here," Money said pulling up to Speedway.

"Ok then, Imma call you tonight," Re Re said. Money disconnected the phone. He walked into Speedway and grabbed a two-liter of Sprite, two cups of ice, and a bag of Jolly Ranchers and walked towards the cash register where he asked if he could get a pack of blunts.

"I don't have a speedy rewards card," he said before she asked the question. He paid and left. He was gone pour up while he trapped and smoked some weed. Pulling back up to Larry's house, he caught the door as Larry came out. *Damn, that shit moving fast,* he thought to himself. He unlocked the door with his keys and when he came through the door, Kia was still on Facebook. He shut the door behind him and locked it. Kia glanced up and saw Money and went back to her phone. He sat at the table putting his drink together.

"Money, why you drink that shit?" Kia asked putting her phone down.

"Why you always on Facebook?" he answered her question with a question.

"Because I like it," she said rolling her eyes because he always had a slick comment.

"Well, I pour up cause I like it," he said rolling his eyes playfully.

"Boy, you a hot mess," she laughed. They spent the rest of the day at the house. At the end of the night, Money dropped Kia off at the hotel before heading out west to see Re Re. When he knocked on the door to her room, she opened it naked. She looked sexy, her chocolate skin was oiled down and her pussy shaved. She pulled him in and secured the door. Dropping to her knees, she unbuttoned his pants and pulled out his rock hard dick and put it in her mouth.

"Damn, Ma, you ain't playing," Money said taking a handful of her hair feeding her his dick. She yanked him out of her mouth.

"When you gone fuck me?" she asked playing with her pussy. Money didn't respond, he just grabbed her head. She understood what that meant. She sucked his balls and jagged his dick off making sure she kept eye contact. He pulled his balls out of her mouth and walked over to the bed slouching down and she followed. She took the oil out of the top drawer and poured it on her titties, and he tittie fucked her nutting all over her chin. The rest of the night was spent fucking.

(MONEY – THE NEXT MORNING)

Money woke up with Re Re in his arms. She was beautiful, but when they first met, he didn't find her attractive. She wasn't the best looking woman, but her personality made up for her looks. He felt guilty cheating on Angel after she held him down all these years. He removed his arm from under Re Re and went to take a shower. After undressing he stepped in the shower and let the hot water relax him. Ten minutes later, he stepped out and put back on the clothes from yesterday. When he walked out the bathroom, Re Re was laying on the bed in deep thought.

"You good, Ma?" he asked.

"Ya, I'm ok," she said staring up at the ceiling. She felt like her world was capsized by Money in one night. She was a little too carefree with her emotions, forgetting the plan was to use him for money. It was easy to fall for him. He had charisma and swag that was irresistible. He came over and sat next to her.

"What's on yo mind?" he asked, seeing something was bothering her and that she seem worried.

"Nothing, I'm good," she said once again, this time sitting up in bed. He stared into her eyes looking for any sign of dishonesty, but saw none.

"I want you to stay down here today," he said putting a smile on her face. She was surprised he wanted her to stay. She thought their relationship was based on sex. Even though they texted each other, that was all he talked about.

"Stay down here and do what? Stay in this room?" she asked already knowing all about his relationship. What man in his right mind would ride around with his mistress?

"Shopping," he answered, going in his pocket and pulling out a stack of money handing it to her.

"Imma make some runs and get up with you tonight," he said standing up to leave. She flashed him a shy smile before he walked out the door. Money hoped the five bands would cheer her up. Re Re got outta bed and took a shower. She thought about last night as the water ran over her body. She still could feel him inside her guts, so deep. He spread her legs wide and massaged her thighs. She was so aroused that when he finally entered her, she came instantly. He worked it all over her pussy, giving her one orgasm after another. She stepped out the shower and got dressed. Even though her plan was working, she felt empty inside. All the years of using men for money were coming back to haunt her. Maybe this was God's way of paying her back for all the years of sinning. Once she was dressed, she used her GPS to find the West Town Mall where she spent the five bandz on everything she wouldn't be able to afford on her own. After spending hours shopping, she made her way back to the motel. Her mind was all over the place, she didn't know what her game plan was. In Money she saw perfection. Ever since the first time she gave him head, she daydreamed about being his woman. What was happening to her, she wondered. She wasn't the romantic type and didn't believe in love. She represented everything evil about women, using sex to get what she wanted. When they met, all she saw was dollar signs. Now her heart was playing tricks on her, and she couldn't understand. She walked over and put a towel under the door, then flamed up a pre-rolled blunt. She laid down and smoked, hoping to clear her mind of all these crazy thoughts. How could she fall for a man she only knew for a week? She'd spent months using men and never felt anything. There was something different about him she couldn't explain. She didn't understand him and it was driving her crazy.

Chapter 6

RE RE, THURSDAY MORNING

*R*e Re woke up the next morning alone. Money never made it, and she fell asleep after masturbating thinking about him. She wasn't about to sweat him, so she packed her things and headed home. When she walked inside the house, her sister and LoLo were on the sofa making out. LoLo broke their kiss.

"What's good Thotianna," he said.

"Boy, find you some business," Re Re said closing the door and walking to her room. She wasn't in the mood to be playing with LoLo's ass today. She laid on the bed wondering what went wrong. Why wasn't Money responding to her like most men. She was used to manipulating men, using her pussy and good head to exploit their weaknesses. She picked up her iPhone and called her best friend, Kim, for advice. Kim answered on the first ring.

"Hi, Girl," Kim said.

"What's good, Girl," Re Re said in a sad voice.

"What's wrong, Bitch?" Kim asked with sympathy.

"I met somebody," Re Re said using the same tone.

"That's good, Bitch. So what's the problem?"

"I don't know really. I guess I like him," Re Re said.

"Oh, and that's fucking with your head? Girl, it's about time you stop acting like a hoe," Kim joked.

"I know, right?" Re Re laughed and sat up in bed. "The only problem is he got a girl," she added.

"That's the story of yo life Girl, you don't want em unless they do. So what makes this one any different?" Kim asked, shaking her head. Re Re was the type of woman who only went for the wrong guys. She always found herself liking the next woman's man. Kim was older and tried to show her the way, but no matter how many times she talked to her, Re Re always made the same mistake again.

"Girl, I like him, I never wanted anything from them other niggas but cash and dick. But I wanna be with this one." Kim heard the pain in her girl's voice and felt sad for her.

"What should I do?" Re Re asked. She was upset with herself for letting good dick get the best of her.

"Girl, I don't know, I'm not the person to be asking cause I can't even keep a man myself. You need to talk to yo sister," Kim said keeping it one hundred with her. She wasn't able to keep her baby daddy from breaking her heart. He was fucking everything in Beloit, making a fool outta her. It took her a year to move on. She hated him with a passion. He hadn't been to see their daughter since she left.

"Ya, you right Girl. Imma call you later," Re Re said.

"Ok, Girl," Kim said hanging up. Re Re went to use the bathroom. She washed her hands and went up front to talk to Lisa, but she wasn't there. On her way back to her room she heard moaning. *Shit*, Re Re thought, *all they do is fuck.* She heard her iPhone ring in her room. By the time she reached it, she missed the call. It was Money. She slung the phone on the bed. She wasn't going to return his call. *Nah, fuck him,* she thought before laying down.

(MEANWHILE – MONEY)

Money sent a text to Re Re from inside his rental. *I'm sorry ma.*

He understood why she was upset. He didn't plan on sending her off when he asked her to stay, but his guilt wouldn't let him return. He waited 10 minutes for a reply but didn't receive one. He placed his phone in his pocket before pulling off. Kia was at the spot, so he had some free time. He rode around taking in his city. At times he wished he never met Re Re. He didn't have time to be wasting time fucking off with a thot. But there was something addictive about her head game, he couldn't get enough of it. He drove past Pen Park and saw all the bum ass block boys outside. They were the only people standing in the cold just to be around each other. Most street niggas in Madison was try'na run through a check, but not them they were cool being broke. He gazed out the window and shook his head, he felt sorry for them. He turned up Cash Moody's song "The Team" and slowed down for them to hear it.

"It was worthless, it was all worthless, the feds drug money LV we purchase. It's all good, shit it serve that purpose. Life is a game, everyday is a circus, rest in peace CJ boy the team still hurting, heaven or hell see you again in person. Getting kushed out before class was the subject throwing money at the teacher why she teaching like

fuck it, it's nothing. Everyday was Christmas, nights turn to Hallow-een. 24/7 nights when I couldn't sleep, I was ambitious through a bad dream. Vision nightmares Picasso couldn't paint the scene. One thing promise hard times is a given, another thing to age is just a time limit. When I'm gone remember how I came in it, newborn fresh no abortion clinic."

They looked back and forth try'na find out what he was on. He smiled and pulled off after flexing on them. He headed back out west to the spot. When he marched into Larry's house, Kia was sitting on the sofa looking good enough to eat. She was wearing a red Louis Vuitton polo shirt and some white skinny jeans with red Chanel heels. Her hair was down and she was holding a stack of cash.

"What's good, Ma?" he asked, closing the door behind him.

"Nothing, try'na run through this check," Kia answered happily laying the money on the table. Money walked over taking a seat next to her.

"What we do?" he asked.

"That's five bands right there, that's all," she said.

"Shit, that's good," Money said flaming up a blunt. He laid back and thought about his future. Yeah, things were gone be aight.

(TWO DAYS LATER)

Over the next two days, things got insane at the spot. They had to do shifts so they could get some sleep. Kia was a trapper, and Money admired her work ethic. She went harder than most niggas. They were staying on the west side at the Best Western hotel off of Gammon Road every night since Kia decided to get her own room. She didn't feel comfortable sharing a room with him. They moved all the work, and shit was really looking great. When it was time to re-up, Money wanted to meet the connect, but she told him he only wanted to do business with her. He understood the game, and saw she didn't trust him. He hoped to change that with time. But if it didn't, the product was so solid, he was willing to continue doing business like that. He gave Kia the $18,000 to show good will with hopes it would help her see he wasn't a snake. She was speechless, no one had ever done anything like that for her. He told her to go back to the Mil and get $210,000 from Angel for three keys.

"You don't mind if we mess around, right?" Kia joked. Within the last 5 days, they had built a friendship.

"Right now you fighting me, but you gone be mine. So that's your pussy too. Just know I ain't one of them lames from yo past. I love Angel with all my heart, but I would never get jealous over her messing with a woman. That's for lames, Ma, not me," he said. His confidence was making her fall for him.

"I was just playing," she said, trying to sound convincing.

"No you wasn't, now go have fun."

(TWO HOURS LATER IN MILWAUKEE)

Kia knocked on the door, Angel opened it, and they stared into each other's eyes. Kia really missed her. They hugged and kissed showing their affection.

"Bitch you must've missed me," Angel said as Kia came into the house.

"You know I missed you, Bitch." They broke into laughter.

"Girl, did Money call you?" Kia asked.

"Yeah he did, the money's upstairs," she said, leading the way to retrieve it. When they made it up stairs, Angel gave her the duffle bag. It was still inside the bag Cash gave them. Kia peeked inside and saw the most money she'd ever laid eyes on.

"Girl, I'm coming to Madison with you. Imma let Tim run things at the club, that's what he gets paid for anyways," Angel told her.

"Did you ask yo man?" Kia asked since she didn't want to risk messing things up with Money. He confided in her a lot and she knew he didn't want Angel anywhere near the game. As a matter of fact, it was one of his rules. Keep your wife at home and out the streets.

"Bitch, you with me or Money?" Angel asked, playing on Kia's loyalty.

"You," she said without hesitating.

"Ok then."

"Whatever, I gotta meet the connect anyway, and Imma be back to get you."

"Ok," Angel said. She was going to be with her man. He'd been gone for five years, and they only spent three days together before he left again. She wasn't having that shit.

"Wait, Kia before you leave, did you fuck Money?" Angel asked.

"No, it's only business with us. He a real nigga, but I'm about this paper," she said feeling bad for lying to her girl. She hadn't fucked him but she played with his dick on two occasions. "I'd be lying if I said I didn't want to, I wish we would've fuck before talking business."

"Girl, you crazy," Angel chuckled.

"Well, Bitch, I gotta make this move. Be ready when I get back."

After leaving the house Kia called the connect informing him she was done with the work. She needed three more, but he wasn't trying to talk business. He wanted to see her again. She was the only thing on his mind after putting that bum head on him, he couldn't stop thinking about her. Kia told him she would see him soon, but right know she had a lot on her plate. He was furious but wasn't trying to show it. He asked if she could handle that much product. She said, "Yeah."

"Ok, but don't forget, this business," he said. Kia went to her house to meet his peoples. She gave them 50 Gs for the last brick and got the other three fronted to her. She put up $43,000, she profitted off this move, putting the rest of the money up to pay later. She felt anguish for deceiving Money after he gave her the profit off the last move, but it was part of the game. Once the work came, she left to pick up Angel. When she pulled up, Angel was outside waiting. *This bitch on it,* she thought. Angel got in and kissed Kia on the cheek.

"Bitch, get off me," Kia said playfully wiping her face.

"Bitch, don't do me," Angel said and kissed her again, this time on the lips, and then Kia pulled off.

"I hope Money ain't upset about you coming up here."

"You let me worry about him," Angel said hooking her iPhone up to the AUXcord to play music.

"Come on girl, I know you don't think Imma listen to slow jams for 45 minutes," Kia said. She hated slow jams because she wasn't the emotional type .

"Bitch, quit complaining," Angel shot her the evil eye.

"*Is it something I did, or is it something I said, is it something you heard, is it something that I'm missing. Tell me what's going on, baby where did we go wrong.*" Dondria's voice came through the speakers. For the last few days, Angel had felt something was wrong with Money. She didn't have a reason to believe he was cheating, but she had a gut feeling. She didn't plan on losing her man after waiting on him five years. She was prepared to do anything to keep him.

"*Baby let me know something, cause I don't understand, I love you and I'm willing to fix this any way I can, but you gotta tell me what's going on, why do you treat me this way, I wanna know where I went wrong.*" She was in her feelings, so she turned the music down.

"Do you love me?" she asked Kia. Kia looked at Angel, interested in where this was coming from.

"Yeah, why?" she asked.

"Because I'm really in love with you and Money, and I don't wanna live without y'all. I never loved anyone other than Money my whole life. And I never expected to feel this way about you," she said laying it on thick. Yeah, it was true, she Loved Kia, but if Money had a problem with it, she would've ended it. Angel wanted Kia and loved Money. It was essential to have the best of both worlds. Kia could be stubborn when her mind was made up, and Angel wanted to have her first threesome tonight. So she need to change Kia's mind, and that was her scheme tonight.

"You don't have to choose between us, Money said it's ok if we mess around," Kia said. She didn't want Angel to feel she had to choose because she believed she would pick Money.

"He only saying that so he can cheat on me," she said and began to cry. Kia remembered the day Money hung the phone up when she walked in on him. She thought he might've been on the phone with another female because he didn't have a problem coming on to her behind Angel's back. She would do anything to make Angel happy.

"Why are you crying, Girl?" Kia asked.

"Cause I love ya'll and I want both," she shouted, confessing her true feelings. Kia thought about what Money said to her today. She couldn't keep lying to herself, she had it bad for him. She took her eyes off the road and looked at her friend and lover.

"I'm about to break a big rule of mine for you, I just hope this don't come back to bite me in the ass," Kia said, showing her devotion.

(2:00 A.M. MONEY'S ROOM)

Money was asleep when he heard a knock at the door. He jumped up, rushing to answer in case it was Kia.

"Who?" he yelled, getting the shock of his life when he found out it was Kia and Angel. They were laughing and having a good time. When he opened the door, he wondered if they'd been drinking. They came inside closing the door behind them.

"Where my work?" he asked, he didn't play when it came to business.

"All business, that's what I like about him," Kia said.

"It's in the room," Angel said. It was obvious he was upset.

"So y'all was drinking traveling up here with my shit?" he asked pissed.

"What? Come on, you ain't the only one that do this," Kia said, feeling herself. "We dropped the work off hours ago, then went out to have a few drinks."

He relaxed a little after hearing them out, but he was still upset Angel rode in a hot car. But they arrived safe and sound, so he let it go. Kia stared at his boxer briefs, his dick was on hard from waking up.

"I knew you had a big dick," Kia said glancing at him.

"Bitch you know because I told you all about it," Angel said licking her lips walking over giving him a kiss. She whispered in his ear, "Don't be mad at me, Daddy. I really missed you. I came all the way up here to make you happy," she said rubbing his dick. "You know I would do anything for you, even share this," she said grabbing his manhood. Kia walked over and kissed the back of Angel's neck.

Angel broke the kiss saying, "Show him you're mine, I wanna watch you suck his dick." Kia was drunk, but even if she hadn't been, she would've done anything for her. She advanced towards him and rubbed his dick before pulling it out. She bent down. He knew he'd end up fucking Kia. He felt like a boss having his girl lover about to give him head. It don't get no better than this. But what really turned him on was how suddenly Kia changed her mind. He'd been trying to fuck her all week, and she acted like he was forbidden. He loved the power Angel possessed over her. He knew one day she'd give into him as well. Kia moved her hair out her face, then took his dick into her mouth. She began to suck the head of it while using her hand to pump the shaft.

"Shit," he said from the sensation of her warm mouth. She ran her tongue down his cock and begin sucking his balls. Angel was so wet from watching, she dropped to her knees.

"Let me help you with daddy dick," she said. Kia pulled him from her mouth letting Angel take control. Angel rubbed it over her face still staring into Money's eyes as she smacked herself on the cheek with his cock, putting it to her lips sucking on it before stopping to give Kia a passionate kiss. Their lips parted and Angel pushed his dick between them. They licked and shared him. He was in paradise. He stopped them before he nutted, pulling his dick away.

"What's wrong?" they asked.

"Shit, take off them clothes Imma fuck the shit outta y'all."

They got up. "Ok, Daddy, first she gone put on a show for you," Angel instructed. Kia begin to dance very provocatively to the music in her head and she undressed as she continued to sway to her own beat until she was undressed. Money and Angel laid on the bed enjoying the show. He saw Kia's fat pussy and couldn't wait to hit that.

"Get over here and put the pussy on my face," Money said, and she did as she was instructed. Angel stood up and got naked and sat on his dick. Kia was bucking and moaning as he ate her pussy.

"Shit, oh shit, suck my clit," she said as her body rocked with excitement. She grabbed the back of his head, pulling him close. "That's it! Shit it feel so good," she was going crazy. Money sucked her pussy until she was shivering and tingling all over, she was loving every minute of it. She felt her clit grow and her cunt get wetter. She had her pussy sucked by both men and women, but nobody came close in comparison to Money. He was the best hands down. His tongue was absolute magic, she could comprehend how Angel fell in love. She pulled his hair cummming with a shudder, soaking his face with her juices. She collapsed on the bed and watched Angel ride his cock. Angel rode him slowly. It wouldn't be long before she came. She glanced into his eyes and saw he was ready to nut, so she hoped off him.

"I wanna watch you fuck her, Daddy," Angel said anxious.

"Yes," Kia screamed, she was in a trance. "I wanna feel that big dick."

Money got on top of her and started to bury his dick inside her. He entered slowly because of her tightness. He tried to give her a second to get accustomed to his size but she didn't want it.

"Please fuck me," she urged him, and he begin to jackhammer her pussy. Kia moaned loudly, bucking her hips while Money held both of her legs straight out and vigorously humped her.

After another minute or so, she finally said, "Money, don't tease me. Give me that dick." He stopped for a second to put her legs up on his shoulders, then he leaned forward onto his hands. By now Kia was screaming, "Don't stop! Fuck me, baby. Come on, fuck me!" In all her years of fucking, she never talked dirty like this. Money really started to pound into her. After every thrust he took his cock all the way out, then slammed it home as hard as he could. The sight of his dick and balls slamming into her was the most exciting thing Angel had ever seen. She laid back playing with herself as she watched her man have sexual intercourse with her lover. It really turned her on, and she begin to have an orgasms. Money wanted to nut, but he understood he needed to fuck Kia good to put her on the team.

"Oh God, this feels so good," she said as she came to a violent orgasm. It felt like she would never stop cumming, he was hitting all the right spots.

"Keep fucking her," Angel encouraged him.

"Shit, it's too good," Kia said having back to back orgasms, and this time Money couldn't hold back any longer as they cum together filling her up with semen. As soon as he pulled out, Angel wrapped her mouth around his dick sucking and licking him clean. When she finished with him, she turned her attention to Kia. She buried her face in her nest putting her tongue in her pussy. She loved the taste of both of them mixed together. They took a rest for a few hours and then fucked for the rest of the night.

Chapter 7

KIA, THURSDAY 11:00 A.M.

*K*ia woke up in Money's arms. Last night was excellent, she never experienced anything like it before. She didn't fathom she could cum so much, he knew just how to stroke her to drive her insane. She went a long time without having a man. She really prayed this didn't interfere with business. She tried to be optimistic about last night, but felt like she played herself for Angel. She really loved her and was devoted to making her happy. She looked at Money and found him staring at her. Angel was laying in his other arm.

"You ok, Ma?" he asked as she looked troubled.

"I'm good, I just don't want this to change things with us being business partners."

"Look, Ma, you my business partner no matter what. Nothing's going change that. I been wanting to fuck you since I first laid eyes on you. No disrespect but I knew you wanted me too. I told you I wasn't like them niggas from your past, this as real as it gets, Ma. And I know you not really into niggas but both of y'all going to be my girls." Angel wasn't asleep, she was laying there listening to the conversation taking place. She opened her eyes and glazed at both of them before smiling. Last night she wasn't sure if this would work, but after having Money fuck her as Kia suck her clit simultaneously, she knew she needed them together. She looked into Kia's eyes and couldn't tell what she was thinking, so she asked.

"What do you think? Was the dick good enough to try it again?"

"Yeah, I liked it but I don't know about being yo Bitch" Kia said. She grabbed Money's dick and started to play with it letting them know she wanted more.

"Girl, you need to stop playing and be with us," Angel said sliding down below the covers to give him head. They went back at it, fucking for hours. Then it was time to get back to business, Angel went back to Milwaukee. Money didn't want her around the trap. Money and Kia talked after everything and she decided she wanted to be friends, nothing more than sex. Money respect her choice because he knew she had trust issues with men. He wasn't the type to force himself on a woman. He knew she would be his before it was all said and done.

(MEANWHILE – CASH)

Today was one of them days most niggas remained in the house, but that wasn't Cash. Every day he woke up and hit the streets no matter what. He loved being alone in his house, but hadn't found a woman valid enough to wife. He was at the crib he got for his team to stay at. He didn't want them in the hood all the time. He came over to see what they was on. For over a hour they sat around talking shit. He was doing most of the jacking, talking about what happened at the club a week ago.

"I know he didn't think he was gone come home to me play-ing his little nigga, never that, I run this motherfucker and guess what?" he asked. "I'm gone buy that lil club just to show him what real money looks like." he said feeling himself. His team laughed, gassing him up. It was necessary to show Money up at all costs. That's all he thought about since he came home. He remembered the day they split up the team. They always had different styles when it came to business. Still, they split everything down the middle when the work was gone, but they didn't have the same bank account. Money believed in saving for hard times, but Cash on the other hand was flaunting, spending every dollar he made and coming to Money for loans. Money wanted him to slow down because his flashy ways brought heat from police, but Cash was his own man and was doing him. Money told Cash if he didn't slow the fuck down, he would stop fucking with him. He felt Cash was gone get them fed time. Cash wasn't trying to hear that and brushed him off. When Cash went to Miami and rented a Lambo-rghini for his birthday and came through Madison telling people he owned it, Money went crazy confronting Cash, which lead to an argument. After the confrontation they both went their separate ways. There relationship hasn't been the same since. Who would've known Money was the hot one. When his brother was locked up, he became his motivation. Everyday he was grinding with payback on his mind. He was done being the Batman to his big brother, Superman. Cash didn't hustle for the money as much as he hustled for the fame. He loved being a boss, having people willing to kill for him, and bitches willing to do anything to be with him. He cherished that power. Cash spent most of his time in Chicago. He still considered it home. Unlike Money he hadn't forgotten where he came from. He loved 35th and State, even though the buildings were gone. They came from nothing they didn't have shit until they started selling drugs. The day their parents found out, they dis-owned them, cutting all family ties. Cash made millions of dollars, and they wouldn't even let him buy them a home. His mom told him his drug money was no good. He loved his parents, but he wasn't ready to give up the fame.

"Yeah I was gone knock his shit in," June said snapping him from his memory.

"Yeah that's why I came here, you lil niggas threw me off. I need y'all to put in some work in Beloit. It's this nigga down there who seem to have forgotten he needs to pay for the work I fronted him. I need that taken care of ASAP."

"That's all you need?" June asked, grabbing his 40. "I got it, I been wanting to put in work since yo brother got me in my chest," he said. He still couldn't get over Money putting his hands on him, he rushed out the house. Cash was proud to see one of the captains of his team always ready for action.

(4 HOURS LATER, BELOIT, JUNE)

"How the fuck they getting money up here?" June thought. Looking out the window, Beloit looked like a town that used to lynch niggas back and the day. He wasn't with this small town shit, and planned on leaving ASAP. He cruised up Poter Avenue with his mind on finding his victim and executing him. He cherished this part of the game and loved taking lives. He got off on killing people. Up ahead he spotted the vehicle he was looking for, with his victim standing in front of it, using the phone. He said a prayer to Lucifer for making his job this easy. He parked behind him and looked at the photo on his phone to be certain he had the right person, and he did. He took a deep breath, slowly opened the door, dude peeked at June as he stepped outta the car, noticing his baby face. He brushed him off, thinking he was just a kid, he looked down at his phone to respond to a text message without a care in the world. June paraded over to him with his heart pounding in his chest, he wasn't scared, and he looked forward to putting in work. His victim was constantly receiving messages from his thots, which drew all of his attention to his phone. He glared up surprised that he was starring down the barrel of a 40. "Cash said keep that money, he wants you to pay in blood." He tried to snatch his gun from his waist, but it was too late.

Bloc!

The ball of fire melted into his forehead, and his head flung backwards from the impact, he tumbled on the hood of the car before hitting the ground. June stood over him. Boc! Boc! He put two more in his head watching as his brains splashed against the pavement, then rushed back to his car. When he made it, someone came sprinting out of a white house with an AK 47. June knew better than to let him shoot first, so he aimed his pistol with a two-hand grip and let off four rounds. Boc!Boc!Boc!Boc! Only one found a home in the middle of his face killing him on impact. The other three shells hit the porch as his body tumbled back, and the AK fell outta his hand. He was dead before crashing to the ground. June hopped in his car and sped off.

(LATER THAT NIGHT IN CHICAGO)

June pulled up to his block on 24th and Normal (Lamron) as Chef Keef, Lil Durk, G.B.E. and OTF niggas called it, but to him it felt like the inferno. Just looking at the four-story building made him sick to his stomach. If you glanced around all you saw was misery; everybody around was poor. June was what people called sexy but deadly. He wasn't the tallest person around, he stood 5'10" and wore his dreads pulled to the back. He was light-skinned and that's what attracted the women. I guess you could say the light-skinned niggas was winning. What got him the most pussy was his body count, he was a well-known hitter. He was a cold killer, and he just murdered someone an hour ago, but it had no affect on him whatsoever. All he was going to do was put two more six-point stars on his chest, as soon as he got up with his tattoo man. He was tatted up and it complimented his thuggish look. He'd been fucking with Cash ever since he was 16 years old. After two years of working for him, he was starting to get frustrated because he wasn't getting any real money. Cash paid them five bands when he wanted somebody killed, but sometimes they went months without work. Shit, he was try'na get paid like Cash, and waiting around to body a nigga wasn't going to work. He wanted to accomplish something to get his family out the hood, cause living in Chiraq, niggas don't give a fuck how many bodies you had because they executed niggas too. He understood why Cash didn't want his young killas selling drugs, because he didn't want them jeopardizing their freedom. June was starting to understand that Cash was an imposter. He acted like he had love for them and made sure they stayed fresh. That was enough to make some loyal to him, but not June. Cash installed some level of fear in him, but it wasn't enough to make him blind to the fact he was being manipulated. He used to be loyal to Cash, but now the only thing he was loyal to was his block. Putting money in his niggas' pockets was his only goal. He hopped out his car with his hands on his 40 with a 30 clip and fear of getting caught lacking as he ran up to the building and opened the door. He took the stairs to his floor and unlocked the apartment door, gun still in his hand. Even though this was his hood, the streets ain't loyal. Any day somebody could come and snatch yo last breath away.

"Who the fuck slamming my door?" his moms yelled from her room.

"It's me, June," he said back.

"Ok Baby, you aight, is everything fine down there?"

"Ya Ma, I'm good, I got the money for the rent too," he assured.

"Ok Baby, thanks, I knew you would come through."

He went to his room and flopped down on the bed, he had a long day and he needed some sleep. Before going to bed, he called his lil bro to make sure he was ok. He picked up his iPhone and FaceTimed him. Once he picked up, June saw he was still at the spot with the team.

"You good, Bro?" he asked, looking at young Killa.

"Ya I'm cooling," he replied. It was easy to see he was high.

"You in for the night, Lil Bro?" June wondered.

"Ya I'm in for the night, love Bro," he told him.

"Love you too," June said meaning every word. June and his brother knew the game they were playing. They understood the streets only intensified the longer you were in them, so they went through drastic measures to make sure they showed their love to each other. With that out the way, he fell asleep.

Chapter 8

JUNE, FRIDAY IN CHICAGO AT 10:00 A.M.

June was busy washing his face. Last night he got some much-needed rest and now he was ready to put a plan together. He needed to get his bandz up, yesterday he saw an opportunity to get in where he fit in. Beloit was open for the taking, after he butchered the biggest drug dealer up there. Cash would be looking for a replacement in the upcoming months. His strategy was to take one of his lil mans up there with him to be his face. It would have to be someone with no connections to the block. Cash would be looking for the nigga with the strongest hustle to be his replacement, and June planned for it to be his mans Fat Boy. Fat Boy was a hustler by every means of the word. He sold whatever he got his hands on, but he wasn't a killa, and in the Windy City that meant you didn't eat. Niggas robbed him every time he got on his feet. Down in Chiraq the weak was food. June didn't fuck with Fat Boy every day, but they were familiar with each other. June was not the type to prey on the weak, so he never fucked with him. Only a "what's up" here and there. But today he would have a conversation with him, about making this move and putting him on. His plan was to let Fat Boy do the trapping, and he would put his murder game on the hustlers, taking everything they had. Today would be a valid day; all he needed to do was find Fat Boy. He spent the rest of the day driving around looking for him. There was no sign of him in the hood. June was starting to get pissed because time wasn't on his side. He went back to the block. He hopped out the car to kick it with his nigga.

"Let me hit that," he asked Rock who passed him the blunt. He toked on it.

"You seen Fat Boy?" he asked standing next to the building.

"Nah, I ain't seen his scary ass," Rock said glancing up the block.

"Man, ain't nobody seen this nigga," June said passing the blunt back to Rock.

"Why you looking for that hoe ass nigga?" Rock asked standing up.

"I just need to holla at him, but let me get up outta here Bro. Make sure you stay on point too. Them G-boys gone retaliate for them bodies y'all dropped the other day," June said to his mans.

"I already know," Rock reassured him showing his 9MM with a 50 round drum. June shook up and left. He needed to find Fat Boy soon.

(MEANWHILE – CASH)

Outside of one of the finest estates available in Chicago, Cash sat inside his car. His highrocks featured gated access to a large private 3.6-acre lot with stunning views. The house is ultra quality and features. Multiple stone fireplaces, water features, and a custom dream kitchen to die for. Cash stepped out of his 2016 Dodge Charger, holding a duffle bag in one hand and his 9MM in the other hand. This was a nightly routine when he came home for the night. He had to stay on point with the war against the GDs. He really hoped to end it soon, but it was only heating up. Once he made it safely in the house, he put the money in his safe and laid down on his bed. The worst part about being a street nigga was you could never really rest. He looked over his shoulder everywhere he went, never being able to trust a soul. The only person he trusted was his brother, but they weren't on speaking terms. He was wrong for acting the way he did with him and he knew it, but his pride wouldn't let him apologize. He wanted to hang with his brother, but his ego was in charge of him. He was on his high horse, but the money that brought him happiness was killing him inside at the same time. He was alone and all the money in the world couldn't buy him loyalty. He fell asleep with a heavy heart.

(SATURDAY)

Cash woke up feeling like new money. All the sad thoughts from yesterday were gone. He washed his face and brushed his teeth before taking a quick shower. He threw on some Fabric-Brand slim fit jeans, a blue and red Gucci polo with some blue Gucci shoes to go along with his B.O.M. sweatshirt. He was on his way to Madison to meet up with Slim Cash and Cash Moody about investing in B.O.M., an up and coming rap label. Moody's mix tape "The Cash Effect" was one of his favorite coming out of Wisconsin. An hour later he pulled up on Rimrock. Slim Cash was waiting outside for him with a hoodie on looking cold as hell. He stepped out of his Charger and shook up with him.

"What's good, Skud?" Slim asked, leading the way into a small apartment building.

"Same shit, Skud, coming to fuck with y'all." They walked up the stairs into the apartment. Inside there was a group of niggas smoking. He said what's up to everybody before going to the back where a room was set up like a studio. Moody was in the booth doing his thing. Slim and Cash took a seat on the leather sectional positioned in the far corner.

"This nigga hot," Cash said shaking his head to the music. He'd learned about Moody watching a video on World Star called "The Team." This was Cash's theme song when he was coming up. He contacted Slim on Facebook to set up a meeting.

"So what's good, Bro?" Slim asked flaming up a pre-rolled blunt.

"Man, I want to invest 100 Gs in Bagz Of Money. I like what I see, and it don't hurt that y'all some of the guys," he said smiling, and they shook up.

"What percentage you try'na get for that?" Slim asked raising his eyebrows.

"Just 20 percent, Skud," Cash said nonchalantly looking Slim in the eyes. Slim pulled from the blunt and passed it to Cash.

"That sounds good to me," Slim said as he blew out the smoke.

Cash stood up. "I got the money, right now in the car."

"Nigga, you riding around with a 100 Gs on you?" Slim asked.

"That light, Skud, no lie," Cash said nonchalantly passing him the blunt back. Slim followed Cash to his car and he gave him the duffle bag full of money.

"Imma have my lawyer get at you about the paperwork," Cash said sitting in the car.

"You do that, hit my line anytime if you got any questions," Slim said looking in the bag. *This what I call Bagz of money,* he thought.

"Ah, Bro, I expect you to be a man of your word. I don't play when it comes to my money," Cash badgered, closing his door and giving him a look that could kill.

Slim laughed inside before saying, "I gotcha." Cash pulled off feeling great about his investment.

(TWO HOURS LATER)

Cash pulled up on Larmon looking for June. The past two hours he tried reaching him but didn't get an answer. When he pulled through, it looked like a ghost town. There wasn't a soul out. He gave up and called the four thot bitches he couldn't get enough of. He hadn't fucked two of them, they only sucked his dick but he was cool with that. Growing up he always had issues getting females to fuck. Bitches thought his dick was too fat and didn't want to have sex because they feared the pain. He got used to the rejection, but the bitches that did fuck couldn't get enough of him. He picked up his phone shooting them hoes a text.

"Have the team ready to do this dick," informing them now he was on his way.

(CHICAGO ON THE BLOCK)

The straight drop had the hypes going crazy, and every day shit picked up. Tre Boi and Ryan was running the spot like a well-oiled machine. The money was rolling in. They finished the 100 grams of boy and took all the money they had and got 300 more. June hadn't been to the spot in days. He showed faith in them by letting them do them. So they wasn't gone let him down. Shit with the G-boys was getting outta hand, last week three of the guys got killed.

They were tired of losing homies. At 21, Tre Boi lost so many niggas, he turned into a savage. He was used to getting news every day about someone getting murked. The city streets were cold for a young gangbanger because they were the ones on the blocks. The old heads with money was somewhere laid up with a bad bitch. They didn't have to worry about getting caught at the corner store.

"Ah Bro, you ever get tired of this shit?" Tre Boi asked Ryan.

"Tired of getting this money?" Ryan questioned.

"Naw Bro, of losing niggas every day. While Cash out here riding in foreign and shit. I ain't hating, I'm just keeping it real, we the ones in the field taking chances, Bro." Ryan thought about it. Tre Boi was right. He'd been feeling the same way for a year now. Cash wasn't in the field with them like a real general. That's why everybody respected June. Every day he strapped up and went to war with them. He put his life on the line, time and time again next to his soldiers.

"Ya Bro, I do, that's why I'm grinding so hard now. Try'na get this money up, so we can branch off. I know that's June plan, when it's all said and done. Cash gone be found somewhere dead. If I know June, that's what's gone happen."

"I hope so," Tre Boi said smiling.

"Me too, right," Ryan said scrunching up his forehead. His iPhone vibrated on the nightstand.

"What's good, Skud?" he asked answering his phone.

"Y'all seen Fat Boy around?" June asked with frustration.

"Hell naw, why you looking for dude?" Ryan asked casually.

"I'm working on something for us. And I need him to make it happen."

"I see bro, if I run into him, Imma make sure I call you."

"Cool, love Bro."

"Love," Ryan said and hung up.

"Who was that?" Tre Boi asked.

"June," Ryan said putting the phone on the table. He grabbed a blunt and placed it in his mouth, he held the lighter to the tip and flicked it until it glowed. He inhaled the smoke like a pro. Then he blew it out and laid back, just like he thought June was plotting.

(TWO BLOCKS AWAY)

Blue sat in a used 2014 Malibu. He had 15 bands on him that he took off the dead bodies, and he was rolling up a blunt. He bobbed his head to the music. His 9MM rested under his leg. The day was cold, but the sun was shining bright. He got out the car and went in the gas station. "Let me get 20 on pump 7," he said passing the clerk the 20 dollar bill before leaving. He pumped his gas and got behind the wheel. As he picked up his blunt, he heard someone yell "7414."

He went for his 9MM and a bullet blew pass his face knocking the blunt from his mouth. Glass rained on him. Boc!Boc!Boc!Boc!Boc!Boc!Boc!

The next one slammed into his shoulder. The bullet that followed hit him in the neck, taking his breath away, leaving him hunched over in his seat. The shooter was determined to kill his target, he walked up to the driverside window, readjusted his aim, and fired.

Boc!Boc!Boc!Boc!Boc!Boc!Boc!

All face shots making sure Blue had a closed casket.

Chapter 9

4 - 6 - 16, SATURDAY, TWO WEEKS LATER IN MADISON

Two weeks passed by fast and the trap was doing numbers. Kia and Money made it back to the room. Things were crazy on Allied, but in a good way. They were moving more than a 100 grams a day. Things were working out just fine with being partners in crime. She never dreamed of making $25,000 a day in her life, and now she was getting that without a problem. Ever since the threesome, she had been spending the night with Money, and they would fuck all night long. They were just alike and had conversations about everything, which made Kia start falling for him. He was the kind of man that any woman would appreciate, and the sex made it difficult to stay away from him.

They called Angel every day and hadn't seen her in two weeks, but missed her. Kia received calls from Danjunema, but not about the product. He wanted to see her. She kept putting it off until it was time to re-up. He was upset, but she had other shit to do. The last two weeks they had made over $350,000, and the unacceptable part about it was they kept it in one of the rooms, while they slept in the other room. They still had 1,624 grams left. It would be at least two weeks more before they saw Angel.

"We going work this spot ourselves forever?" Kia asked. She prayed he didn't say yeah, because they would always have to go weeks without seeing Angel.

"Right now we gotta work the house because we don't have a team. It's just the two of us," he expressed.

"I told you from day one, my friends could work and be trusted," she said. He knew this, but he treasured trapping and having money come through his hands. Kia missed seeing Angel; talking on the phone wasn't good enough. They didn't have to work the spot; everything was set up just right.

"You right, Ma, when the rest of this shit gone, we going to put your girls to work. We only need two of them. That's enough people!" " Yeah." "You ready to stop playing?" he asked.

"Who playing?" she asked with a expression of shock on her face.

"You know you can't get enough of me, you sleep with me every night, and I wake up, you be staring at me smiling," he said joking. "What's stopping you from being mine?" Kia thought about everything he said. He was keeping it real, but she would always be the third wheel in their life. They would never cherish her like they cherished each other. She didn't want him playing games with her heart.

"Don't be scared Ma, I got you. Imma take care of y'all, all you gotta do is trust me."

"Imma try, just don't hurt me ok, or else," she said playfully, she was gone give him a chance and put her past behind her. She was scared because she never gave her all to a man. She didn't know if she could take it if he cheated. She wasn't naïve to the fact that his good loving made her fall in love in less than a month. Her emotions were all over the place; she just hoped she wasn't acting on impulse, and he didn't do anything to get himself killed, playing with her heart.

"I got you Ma, don't worry."

Kia got up to call Angel and deliver the good news.

(MEANWHILE – DANJUNEMA)

In the past two weeks he called Kia over 20 times, and she gave him the run around. He didn't like the disrespect she was exhibiting, but he understood it. He thought about it as he set inside the private jet. It was the ultimate international VIP craft, with seating for up to 16 passengers, with a large living room, master bedroom, and meeting room. It allowed him to fly in comfort. He was on his way to LA for a business meeting. His two bodyguards were with him. Gero was tall and black as tar. They met in Nigeria over 20 years ago, were Danjunema witnessed how brutal he could be when he saw Gero slaughter 20 women and children at the command of the army. The next day Danjunema reached an agreement with him to leave the army and work for him. Gero bargained with him to bring along his brother Chipo who showed he was just as cold blooded. Chipo wasn't as tall as his older brother, he was short and fat with dreadlocks hanging down to his ass. Danjunema took them everywhere he went. They were family.

"Boss, is everything ok?" Chipo asked.

"Yes, I'm fine," Danjunema replied, looking down at his computer.

"Can I get you anything, Boss?"

"No, I'm ok, thank you Chipo," Danjunema said going back to work. For the last 20 minutes his mind was overactive with thoughts of Kia. He understood why she was disgusted with him, he wish she found it in her heart to forgive him. It would be a dream come true for him, but he wouldn't hold his breath. Kia's resentment for him ran deep, more than a decade. In his heart he felt what he did was inappropriate and wanted to correct his wrongdoing. He laid back in his seat to take a nap, pondering a way to change the past.

Chapter 10

4-20-16, TWO WEEKS LATER

The last two weeks again went by fast. They packed everything up and went to the mill with $750,000 in the car with them. When they pulled up to the house, Money got out, grabbing the duffle bags, and marched with Kia into the house. Kia hollered for Angel as soon as the door closed. Angel was upstairs when she heard her name being called. She got up and ran down the stairs with only her boy shorts on and wife beater. She walked into the living room, Money was laying cash on the table. Kia ran to Angel and gave her a kiss. They were truly in love, Money thought. Angel broke the kiss and came over and gave Money one.

"Kia, help me split this money up so we can bust these moves," he told her, his mind still on business. Angel was upset she hasn't seen him in a month, but he was acting like he didn't miss her.

"What you don't miss me?" she asked pissed off.

"Come on Ma, you know I missed you. We both missed you," he said giving her a hug. "That's why we ain't going back to Madison, we gone stay here with you. We gone send Kia's friends up there to work the spot." Angel couldn't pretend to be mad any-more. He just made her month because being alone was hell.

"Oh, I'm sorry," she said smiling. "It's cool, Bae, let's count this cash up." It took them over an hour to count the capital. Money took his $210,000 out for the work, and told Kia they both would get $273,000.

"Look, Ma, if we a team this gone be the last time we split any-thing up, if we getting it together, we spend it together."

Kia didn't say anything, she thought about what he said. She saved more than $300,000 in a little over a month. That was more than enough off a partnership with him, so why not see where things went with them.

"Ok," she said. She was really falling for him, she had her guards up for so long, never letting herself trust a man because they weren't trustworthy. But he wasn't like most men, and every-thing he said had significance, he wasn't just running game.

"Then put yo money up, you won't need it as long as you my girl, I'm gone take care of you," he claimed.

"Oh and you moving in with us," he said giving her no choice.

"Ok," she said loving how he made decisions for her, some-thing she never let other men do. He took $210,000 out of his half a million in drug money.

"Kia, we gone need three more bricks," Money said. It hurt Kia to be exploiting him, she wish she never lied about the price of the work, but she couldn't tell him now. She didn't wanna look like a snake so she left it alone. He gave Angel $250,000 to put up. With the odd 63,000 remaining he was going to take them shop-ping. Things were looking up for them, and he'd only been home a month and a half. With Kia on his team, he'd be making $700,000 every 45 days. He couldn't wait to run into Cash and ask who the broke nigga was now. Why he felt the need to prove something to him, he didn't know. He'd been out-hustling him from day one. It had something to do with his brother try'na to show him up.

(KIA)

Kia went through hell when it was time to re-up. She wished she never sucked his dick, but at the time, it felt like the best thing to do. He was starting to act controlling, he told her if she didn't come see him before she re-upped, he would cut her off. She made it back to the house from picking the work up at her crib. She didn't have him front her, she gave him $300,000 - $150,000 for the last three, and paid for three more. She put up the other $60,000 profit. When she made it inside with the work, Angel told her to take it up stairs. They knew better than to keep the product in the house, but thought it was fine because it would only be there tonight.

When she came back downstairs Money asked, "Did you talk to the girls?"

"Money, try saying hi sometimes, you don't always have to get straight to business," Kia said and he laughed because she was right. "But yeah I did, we gone leave in the AM."

He gave her a look and said, "We?"

"Yeah, I'm only going to show them around and give them the lay out. Then Imma be home, Daddy, don't worry." Just hearing her say that turned Angel on, she loved that shit.

"Let's go to Chicago, I want to treat my ladies to a shopping spree," Money said.

(MEANWHILE – JUNE)

Over two weeks had passed and shit was going great at the trap. He paid T-mack the money he owed him and bought another brick. And finally got started on his other plan. He had trouble getting Fat Boy to trust him enough to go outta town. He got so frustrated with dude, he thought about killing him, but figured what good would that do. The way he convinced him was confessing his plan, and after telling him, Fat Boy wanted in. The delay set him back, he desperately needed to make up the lost time. They made it to Beloit two days ago, and that's when he learned his plan wasn't as magnificent as he thought. Their biggest problem was they didn't know a soul up there. So being a thinker, he understood the best way to find out the who's who of any town is linking up with a bitch. But not just any bitch, a street bitch. He hit the streets, he didn't need to look for long before finding one at the Mobile gas station who thought he was attractive. Kim was a sexy red bone, she stood 5'5" and was stacked. Her breast size was 36D with a 26-inch waist and a fat ass. She wore her hair long and it touched her ass. She was 28 years old. She had June by 10 years but still looked beautiful. After only an hour of chopping it up with him they grabbed a bottle of Ciroc and then headed to shawty crib where she had 12 inches of hard dick inside her. The plan was to give her so much cock that she'd tell him everything he wanted to hear in the morning. They'd been fucking for over a hour and he wasn't showing any signs of letting up.

"Damn, Ma, yo pussy dripping wet," June teased as he felt her near an orgasm.

"Yes! Oh Yesss…. Fuck me, yo dick feel… Sooo good," she squealed. She was about to cum. " I'm cumin… Shit….. Fuck…. Meee."

"Yeah, cum all over this dick for me," he said as he picked up his pace hitting the bottom with three inches still showing.

"I can't take no more," she said as her body began to shake and her juices started to run down her leg.

"Then suck it for me, Ma," he asked still fucking her hard.

"Yesss," she moaned out.

"Tell me you love this dick."

"I love it so, soo much," she begin to cry in delight of the best sex she's ever had. He pulled out and she hoped up turning around putting it in her mouth. She licked the head and spit on it, but he was ready to nut so he grabbed the back of her head and began fucking her face.

"Ya, suck this big dick, Bitch, just like that," he said before cumming in her mouth. After swallowing it all, she stood up in went in the bathroom. June watch her fat ass jiggling as she walked. He knew she wouldn't be able to get enough of him. He smiled because things were looking up for him, and his days of putting in work for Cash were coming to an end. All he needed to do was lock down this town. First heads would have to turn and bodies would have to drop, but that was all in a day's work for him. Coming out the bathroom was the ticket to his success. He watched her make her way over to him.

"That was the best sex I've ever had," she said laying on his chest and rubbing his dick at the same time.

"You saying it like you surprised. I told you I was gone beat it up," he said nonchalantly.

"A lot of niggas say that and don't do shit, the dick be weak as fuck."

"Ya Ma, I'm not those niggas, I'm one of a kind. They don't make em like me. So be lucky I chose you to ride for my team. We about to tear shit down and take over this lil town."

"Y'all ain't about to take over shit. These niggas up here ain't going. Cam'ron and his boys ain't having none of that. They lay shit down too." Just like he expected, she started talking, and he planned to listen and learn, then he was going to bring the heat like Dwade. Once he took over this town, he would bring his team up here. He was losing niggas left and right over a war that wasn't getting any of them paid.

(CHICAGO, 11:00 A.M., CASH)

Cash and Yung Killa sat outside on Lamron in Cash's Cadillac XT5 having a conversation. Cash pulled up 10 minutes ago wanting to know where June was. It's been over a month since he'd seen him at any of the spots.

"Bro, I don't know what big bro been on, but he been keeping to himself, only time I hear from him is when he FaceTime me," he said sincerely. Every time he calls June, his calls were ignored.

"See what's wrong with him next time you talk to him, tell him big folks worried about him. I need him to get at me A.S.A.P. I got some shit I need taking care of."

"Cool, I'm gone tell him, but to keep it real, he more than likely laid up with a bitch," Killa said making up an excuse for his brother. It was easy for Cash to see he was lying, he could read the lil niggas like a book.

"Cool then Imma hit you up later," he said shaking up with him before pulling off. Five cars full of killaz on his team followed behind him. The streets were ruthless, and he wasn't about to be lacking. He pulled up looking for June to see if he was still a part of the team because it wasn't his style to just disappear like this. June wasn't like the rest of his young niggas, he had a mind of his own. Cash understood from day one he needed to keep an eye on him. June was born to slay niggas, and had the heart of a lion and boss written all over him. If he put his mind to it, he could take over the streets. That's the main reason he didn't let him in the dope game. He didn't want him having too much money because with money came power. He was going to give June a week to call him, and if he didn't, he'd put the word out to murk him. June wasn't the type of person you wanted as an enemy. They had enough on their plate with the G-boys. It wasn't time to turn against each other.

(MEANWHILE)

Money and Angel were laid up at home. Last night after shopping, Kia and her girls went to Madison. She wanted to demonstrate how things worked. Then she was coming back to be with them.

Angel was happy to have her man home. Yesterday Money took them shopping and they ran him down so much that when they made it home, he fell to sleep, no sex or nothing. She knew how much he hated shopping, but he had fun watching them try on sexy clothes and making out at the same time. His ass was going crazy. Angel planned to wake him the best way she knew how. She went under the covers and pulled his dick out and began to give him head. It didn't take long before he grabbed the back of her head and pushed it down further on his dick. About 15 minutes later she was swallowing his cum.

"Damn, Bae, you sure know how to make a nigga feel like a boss."

"It's my job to take care of you. Because your mine and I love doing it," she said, hopping up to brush her teeth.

"Angel, what we getting in to today?" Money asked, getting outta bed.

"I gotta go to the club and set up for this party Cash Moody having at the club. You should come tonight, everybody gone be there," she said sticking her head outta the bathroom.

"Ya, that club shit really ain't my style. That shit have a nigga feel like I'm suffocating, with all them people around."

"Boy, that's prison talk, yo ass coming with me tonight. I'm try'na show my man off to these bitches and have some fun."

"Fuck it, we there," he said.

Chapter 17

IN MADISON

*O*anjunema sat outside one-eyed Larry's house waiting for Kia to come out. He had enough of her games, and planned to show her who was in charge. He didn't like to be manipulated, and Kia was giving him the run around. It was time she learned her place, he was going to remind her she worked for him. He wished he didn't have to do this because he'd been in love with Kia for 15 years. She didn't have to sell drugs, he'd give her anything her heart desired plus more, but she hated him for taking her virginity the way he did. After years of rejection, he wished he could take it back. He should have reconnected with her and done things different, but back then he never thought he'd fall in love with her. His attraction was lust and he acted on it.

"There she is, Boss, you want them to take her?"

"Ya," he said knowing this wouldn't advance his chance at gaining her trust, but it needed to be done. He was going to stop pursuing for sex and just do business with her, like he would with anyone else. He needed her to understand that lying could get you killed in this line of work.

Kia was walking to her car when a rusted black van came to a screeching halt in front of her. Three masked men jumped out wearing all black. Instantly her survival instincts kicked in. She went for her knife, but wasn't quick enough and got smacked on the side of the head with a gun. She fell, hitting her head on the concrete and blacked out.

When she came to she was blindfolded and tied to a chair. The blindfold got pulled off and there Danjunema sat, across from her.

"Kia, why must I go through drastic measures in order to meet with you?"

"I told you, I been working, Dajunema, damn, I don't have to come running when you call," she yelled.

"Kia, you don't have to hide from me. You know I would never hurt you."

"What the fuck do you call this?" she asked showing the right side of her head.

"They were told to bring you to me unharmed, but I forgot you're a fighter. But so are my men, and they're immaculate at following orders. You're alive and well."

"What, do you want to rape me again?" she asked with a cold expression.

"Rape you I never did, I gave you a choice and you chose to live, but talking about the pass isn't the reason we're here. I brought you here to talk about our future."

"We don't have a future, never have, never will," she said. She hated how he always took her power away from her. He made her feel weak.

"But we do have a future, I'm here to let you know. I'm sorry for making you have sex with me to do business. From this day forward, I will conduct business with you as I do with any other person. I also feel the need to inform you when my other business partners don't pay, I kill them, and the same goes for you my lady. Do you understand?"

"I wouldn't have it any other way," she said mean mugging him.

"Then let's get rich, and again, I'm sorry for our past. I will have my people take you to your car. Understand that they're just doing their job." His man untied her, she stood and walked towards the door.

"You don't want a ride?" Danjunema asked.

"I don't want shit from you," she said walking outta the door. She walked a block before realizing she wasn't in Madison. Damn, she hated him, she thought as she made her way back to his house.

She walked in. "Where the fuck am I?" she yelled.

Danjunema smiled. "Somewhere few walk out of," he said standing to his feet.

"Kia, I'm really sorry for everything. If I could do it all over again, I would." She saw sincerity in his eyes, a pain inside them so deep that a light bulb went off inside her head. Her pussy was on fire as the thought of the power she possessed traveled through her mind, changing her forever. From this day forward she was in control.

"What would you do to make it up to me?" she asked licking her lips.

"Anything," he said invading her space.

"Anything?" she asked putting her hands to his lips and pushing him away. "You can start by taking me back to Madison."

(LATER THAT NIGHT: BELOIT – JUNE)

Kim disclosed to June everything he needed to know to take over. Even where niggas in Cam'ron's team laid their heads. That was the power of good dick. He told her when everything was done, she'd be Wifey. But she was dead the moment he didn't need her. That bitch was gone have to go when everything was in place. He didn't want anything tying him to this town other than Fat Boy. The reason she was willing to give him the info on Cam'ron and his team was her baby daddy worked for him. She hated him for leaving her for the next bitch. She wanted him dead for playing with her heart. June felt the nigga deserved to die for talking so much. This bitch knew all their business because he pillow talked to his hoe. Right now June was outside their stash house waiting on him to come out. She informed him that once a week her baby daddy picked up cash from this house; anywhere from 50 to 100 bandz. He couldn't pass this up, this would put him where he needed to be. After about 10 minutes of waiting, he came out with a shoebox in his hand. June stepped out of his hiding spot in the bushes. He was like a lion on his prey and he never saw him coming. June put two shots in the back of his head. The slug ripped through his brain causing him to flip around. June stood over him and put four bullets in his chest. His dick got hard as the muzzle flashed. BOC!BOC!BOC!BOC! He grabbed the shoebox, then went inside his pockets, taking his car keys. He jumped in the car, making a clean getaway. After parking the car, he walked five blocks to Kim's house. As soon as he made it inside, she jumped in his arms.

"Did you do it?" she asked, happy as hell, and something told him she'd been planning this shit for years.

"Ya, it's done," he said putting her down. He stared into her eyes looking for any signs of sadness.

"How much money did you get, Baby?" she asked. She didn't give a fuck about him killing her baby daddy to get this money. She was the kind of woman he wanted, heartless and cold. He might just put her on the team.

"Let's count it and see."

"No you can. While I suck yo dick," she said licking her lips.

(12:00 A.M. INSIDE Q.O.H.)

Money was inside Angel's office. He was getting some air because the club really wasn't his thing. He picked up his phone and called Kia before taking a seat at Angel's desk.

"What's good Bae? When you coming home?" he asked, putting her on speaker.

"I'm gone be a little longer than I thought. Imma be back in two days."

"Damn, two more days without you? Well I was just checking on you."

"Ya, Daddy, everything fine. I'm at the hotel now and I'm in for the night so I'm straight."

"Ok that's all I wanted."

"Ok then, tell Angel I miss her and call me tonight."

"Cool," Money said hanging up. They hadn't told each other they loved one another. He didn't want to rush things, but he had strong feelings for her. He missed her taking the other spot in bed. He stood up to make sure things were going fine with the party. Everything looked ok other than Cash walking in. He saw Angel point to Cash talking to the head of security. After the conversation, the security guard ran to the front door where Cash stood with his team. The guard stopped them, making sure they weren't strapped. Two of his mans was led out by security. Money went down to make sure everything was fine.

"Everything good?" he asked.

"Ya, everything cool, we just sent them out, they were try'na get in with hammers, that's all boss."

"Good job, Bro," he said before turning around walking to V.I.P. where Cash and his niggas were.

"What's good, Bro?" Cash said, his hand out to shake up with him. Money looked at it but didn't shake it.

"What's good, Nigga. I see you still mad about the shit from last time. You know I wasn't gone let my lil nigga murk you, shit, we still family." Cash smirked putting his hand in his pocket. His team laughed.

"Bro, let this be yo last time coming at me like Imma hoe," Money said getting directly in his face, staring him dead in the eyes. Yung Killa stood up.

"You good, Cash?" he asked.

"Ya, I'm cool, this just my big bro," he said waving him off, and Killa sat back down.

"Y'all must think y'all the only killas," Money said, talking to Killa, but pointing at their whole team.

"Naw we ain't. But I shoot for free, I'll let you have it," Killa said and he wasn't playing.

"Cool out Killa, I said he family. He just ain't with the team."

Money had enough of playing games with Cash. He was going to show them not to fuck with him tonight.

"Y'all enjoy y'all selves," he said before walking away.

"Fuck you too then, nigga," Cash yelled for everyone to hear, and they laughed at his comment.

Money made his way to Angel's office and took the gun out of her desk. He made sure it was locked and loaded. Then he waited over an hour as Cash and his team made it rain on stage with Cash Moody and the B.O.M. gang. He texted Angel telling her to get a ride home from Tim. The club was getting ready to let out in 20 minutes when he slipped out the back door to wait. If he was right, Cash would send someone out first to get the pistols, to make sure he left the club safely. It was something Money showed him growing up. When Killa came walking out, things couldn't have been better. Money waited on the side of Cash's truck. Just as Killa was about to open the door, he stepped out.

"What's good, Lil Nigga," Money said putting the gun to the back of his head. "You ain't talking crazy now." He pressed the cold steel against his dome.

"Nigga, fuck you, do what you gotta do, Pussy," Killa said. He wasn't about to beg for his life. Money was about to blow his shit back when he heard gunshots.

Bloc!bloc!bloc!

He dropped to the ground and Killa took off running. Money let off three shots boom!boom!boom! hitting Killa in the back. He fell as the bullet ripped through his muscular frame. He yelled in pain, crashing to the ground. Money turned around to see who was shooting at him. He glance over the roof of the van and saw the dudes' security abstracted from the club coming his way letting off shots. Bloc! Bloc! Bloc! Bloc! The bullets missed their target, hitting the truck. The gunfire rocked the Range from side to side, riddling it with bullets. He was out numbered and out gunned, so he stayed low, ran to the side of the building, and jumped in his car pulling off.

Chapter 12

ANGEL

Angel was inside the club when she heard gunshots. Everyone stayed inside, but Cash and his people rushed out. The police showed up and ended the party, but the club was closing anyways. She looked all over for Money and couldn't find him. When she picked her phone up, she saw a text across her screen saying *get a ride from Tim.*

"What happened outside?" she asked the head of security.

"Somebody got shot in the lot. Niggas just can't have a good time," he said shaking his head.

"Who the fuck got shot?" she asked, hoping it wasn't Money.

"They don't know. When the police pulled up, they found blood on the ground and a car shot up."

"Ok, close up for me, please. I'm about to get an Uber." Angel took out her phone and called her man. He answered on the third ring.

"Bae, you ok?"

"Ya, I'm good, what made you ask that?" He wasn't telling her something, she heard it in his voice but decided to wait until she got home to ask. She didn't trust phones nowadays. You never knew what the government could do.

"Ok, I love you too," she said wondering what he got himself into. She hated when people did shit at her club, and if he had something to do with it, it was his ass.

(JUNE – MEANWHILE, BELOIT)

June felt good about coming up on 200 bandz. This was the biggest lick he hit, and he celebrated by smoking blunt after blunt of loud and sipping lean with Kim. The more they talked, he began to understand her, and she seemed to be loyal as hell. She was the type of individual that would give you her trust, but once you crossed her, that was it. They had a lot in common, and he liked her style. He picked up his phone to FaceTime his lil bro but didn't get an answer. He tried two more times and still no answer. Something wasn't right because he always picked up for him. June went in the front room and grabbed his car keys.

"I gotta go, something ain't right at the crib," he said moving quickly. His heart was telling him something happened to his lil bro.

"Well, I'm coming with you," she said getting up.

"You can't. Imma be right back," he said grabbing the bag of money. That's when it hit him. She talked too much, so he decided to take her along.

"Get your shit and come the fuck on." He didn't need her jeopardizing his plan and wasn't ready to kill her. He planned on letting her prove her worth. She didn't take long to get ready and they were out the door.

(IN CHICAGO)

They made it to the city at 5:00 a.m. June called Killa over and over without an answer. He pulled up to the house, and the look on Kim's face was priceless.

"You live here?" she asked with a skrew face.

"Ya why? Is that a problem?" he asked seeing where her head was. His mom told him, when a women wants you, she takes everything that comes along with you.

"No, ain't no problem, Baby," she said giving him a kiss on the lips. As he stepped out the car, his phone rang. He looked at the screen, it was his brother calling.

"What's good, Lil Nigga, I been blowing yo line up," he said.

"This Cash, bro."

"What you doing with my brother phone?" he asked pissed off.

"Man, the lil nigga got shot last night at the club. He left his line in my ride."

"He got what? Who shot my brother?" he yelled with frustration and anger, ready to kill a nigga.

"Calm down bro, shit gone get taken care of. We having a meeting tonight at the honey comb hide out," Cash mumbled. June was trying his best to keep his cool so he wouldn't expose his hand. His plan wasn't fully in effect yet. It wasn't time to fall out with Cash yet. First he needed to get his bandz up.

"Aight," he said in a disengaged tone.

"Aight, see you tonight, Bro. Love," Cash added. June didn't reply before hanging up the phone.

"Everything ok, Bae?" Kim asked worried.

"Ya, everything good, we gotta get a room down here for a couple of days, I gotta take care of some business," he said pulling off.

(MEANWHILE – CHICAGO, CASH)

"I can't believe this nigga hung up on me," Cash thought. He didn't know what June was thinking lately. He was acting like he wasn't a part of the team. Cash thought one day this would happen, but not like this. He couldn't think of what made June turn on him. He did everything for him, and this was how he repaid him, with disrespect. June needed to be handled, but deep down in his heart, he wanted to let him do him. June was like a little brother to him, killing him wasn't an option. Tonight at the meeting he would suggest June do his own thing, that's what he wanted anyways. Cash just hoped he wasn't making a mistake.

(LATER THAT DAY – CHICAGO, JUNE)

June walked into his brother's hospital room. When he saw Killa hooked up to those monitors, he lost his mind. Somebody would pay for this, he gave his word to Dave.

"What's good, Big Bro?" Killa asked opening his eyes, happy to see his brother. June was so glad that he survived.

"What's good?" he said walking over to the bedside. "How you feeling, Lil Bro?" he asked.

"Like King David," he said with a smirk on his face that made June smile.

"Yo ass crazy, Bro. So you feeling like a boss after getting shot. That's good you ain't letting this shit keep you down," he said shaking up with him. "Who shot you, Bro?" he asked.

"Man, I don't even know to keep it real," Killa said.

"Tell me what happened," June said taking a seat. Killa told him everything that went down that night, minus who shot him.

"So Meek and Tez save yo life, man that's crazy on Dav. Tell them lil niggas I owe them," he said feeling guilty for not being there to watch his back. He blamed Cash at the same time. They'd been with him from the beginning, and he still played them. He kept them at low level on the team, ain't no way after all these years of putting in work that Killa should've been going to get the straps. A new nigga should've been doing that.

"Bro, shit picking up at the spot so I ain't fucking with Cash like that. I'm on my own shit," June said. Killa's facial expression changed and a look of disappointment flashed across it.

"You on some other shit, how you gone leave the team?" Killa asked.

"What team, Bro? You sound crazy, this nigga the only one eating, and that ain't what a team about. We all should be eating, but he the only one worth millions. We ain't got shit. What you gone do, play that nigga bitch for the rest of yo life, Bro? Well I'm about to do me," June stood up pissed off and ready to leave.

"Fuck Cash and his team, Bro. You need to open yo eyes up," he said and they shook up.

"Love, Bro," Killa said taking in everything that was discussed. He was with getting money on the side but leaving the team, he didn't know about that.

"Love, Bro, everything said in here stays in here too," June said because he wasn't ready to let Cash know how he felt.

"You don't have to tell me no shit like that. Just be safe cuz he ain't gone take you leaving the team too well."

"That's why he ain't gone know," he said walking out the door. Cash would be the last to find out, and when he did, he would die soon after. June hopped in the car with Kim.

"You ok?" she asked.

"I'm good, but Imma need yo help with something."

"Anything for my baby," she said with a smile.

"Ya, that's my girl, always willing to ride for the team."

(MEANWHILE – KIA, MADISON)

"Bitch, you got me fucked up," Kia said. She was at Denny's eating with her girls Ne-Ne and Tay. They were having a conversation about her getting some dick.

"I bet that nigga went crazy when he felt them walls for the first time. How long it's been four years?" Tay asked.

"Ya, girl, that was my first time in a long time."

"Was he mad about you and Angel?" Ne-Ne wanted to know.

"Nah, he a boss, bitch. He told me only a lame nigga would get mad about that shit."

"Girl, you lying?" Tay asked shocked.

"Bitch, if I'm lying, I'm dying," Kia said.

"That's my type of nigga. Do he got some friends?" Tay asked giving Ne-Ne a high five.

"Y'all bitches crazy," Kia said and burst out in laughter.

"But on the real, tell him thanks. A bitch need that 20 Gs a month," Ne-Ne said sincerely. Kia was happy to assist her friends. She wanted to go home, but she couldn't let them see her face. She had a big bump on her head from getting hit with the gun, but it was nothing. She rather get hit than to fuck Danjunema. She despised him and nothing could change that. She didn't understand why he kept trying, but she didn't have a problem with his change of heart.

"I'm happy for you Kia, you look happy since you been getting some dick," Tay said.

"Ya, I knew that bitch wasn't gay," Ne-Ne said, and they all laughed. Kia really missed them. Everything was going great, as far as business. She wanted to conversate with Money about selling weight. She wanted to confess to the price of the work, it didn't feel right getting over on him anymore. But what he didn't know wouldn't hurt him, and it damn sure wasn't hurting her, putting up 60 bandz every time they re-up. Something was changing about her. Her heart was with Money, and she had feelings for him. But there was something about deceiving a man that turned her on. She decided she wouldn't tell him. This was the happiest she's ever been, and she wanted it to remain that way. She prayed that this new feeling of power wouldn't corrupt their relationship.

(LATER THAT NIGHT – CHICAGO, CASH)

Cash and the most loyal members of his team were seated at the round table. There were men from all over the U.S. sitting in this meeting, with only one new person attending – June. Cash couldn't kill June, so he thought it was best to bring him in on the business side of things. He wasn't gone give him much, maybe a block or two, to make him feel important and stay loyal. In front of him sat

250 bricks of coke for his team. All but 10 were sold, and the rest would go to June. That's how much love he had for him. He was gone let him slide on the disrespect. Sometimes being the boss was hard. The meeting didn't take long. Cash knew better than to sit in a room with product. Before everyone left, he told June to stay behind. So they could talk.

"What's good, Big Bro?" June asked.

"I know you got a mind of your own, Lil Bro, and that's why I called you to this meeting. I wanna let you in on the dope game, my nigga, and give you a chance to make some real money. You been with me long enough and showed me your loyalty. So what's good, you try'na get this money?"

"I don't know shit about trapping," June lied. He wasn't new to the game and played his role well.

"All you gotta do is drop the work off to the lil niggas, and when they done, I'm gone pay you 50 Gs. That's it. That's all. Drop it off and pick it up."

"Fuck it, then I'm in," June said. "But what's good with opening a spot on the block," June commented.

"Cool," Cash said, giving him the green light. Cash told him everything about his new block, and then June left with the coke. Cash felt like a lot was accomplished with June running the block. He could keep an eye on him.

After the meeting, Cash made a short drive over to Dria's house to see his "sex team." Dria, Barbie, Lavish, and Lesa were just amazing. He loved to visit them because he got a variety of different women at once. Dria was tatted up from her neck. Her ink was done at 9 Mag out in Chicago. She had a small waist with a big, disrespectful ghetto booty. She was light-skinned and 5'8" tall.

Dria should have been somebody's wife, but she was in love with Cash and his street fame. Barbie was the only one other than Dria he was able to fuck. She was dark-skinned and tatted with 34Ds and a 25-inch waist with 40-inch hips. Her 5'4" frame was to die for. She had the best pussy Cash had ever come across. He stepped out his car and went to the door, unlocking it with the key Dria gave him a week ago. When he walked in, they were sitting on the sofa in the living room. Lavish and Lesa were sitting next to each other, looking through their phones. Cash couldn't wait to fuck. Lavish looked like a model. She was super thick. She reminded him of Ayisha Diaz. Lisa was a spitting image of Erica Mene.

"What's good, Daddy?" Dria asked walking over giving him a hug.

"Shit, Ma, what y'all getting into?" Cash asked.

"Nothing, why? What you got in mind?"

"Shit, I don't know, I came over to relax," he said taking a seat on the couch next to Lavish.

"Well I'm about to run and get some Ciroc," Dria said grabbing her car keys and walking out the door. They sat around for 10 minutes talking on their phones, waiting on Dria to return. Dria came through the door holding two fifths of Ciroc.

"It's time to turn up, Bitches," she yelled closing the door behind her.

"It's about time," Lavish said, standing up for the first time and giving Cash a view of her fat ass hanging outta her shorts.

"Bitch, quit it," Dria said waving her off. Cash stood up and took one of the fifths and popped the top before taking a drink. He sat on the couch and watched the girls devour the Ciroc.

"I hate drinking, Girl, every time I do my pussy get wet," Lavish said staring at Cash. She felt the blood rush to her cunt.

"Bitch, yo ass crazy. We got a nigga with money and a fat dick sitting on the couch, and you talking about you hate getting drunk cause you get horny. I bet all you got to do is ask, and you'll get more dick than you can handle," Barbie said and everybody laughed.

"Bitch, you got me fucked up, ain't no dick big enough to scare me," she said, lying.

"Whatever, you and that bitch Lesa be running from that thing," Dria said hopping in the conversation. They were all drunk, and Cash sat on the couch watching and praying Lavish would fall for the peer pressure.

"Like I said, y'all got me fucked up," she said, walking over to the sofa and sat on Cash's lap. "Come on, I wanna try it," she said standing up and rubbing his cock. Dria and Lesa began taking the pillows off the couch and spreading them on the pool table. Lavish pulled his pants down and began sucking his dick. He watched Dria, Barbie, and Lesa undress while Lavish laid him on the pool table. She had him lay on his back, then got up, undressed, and straddled his cock. Barbie came over and spread her cunt over his face. Lavish was having a hard time taking more than an inch of him inside of her. She was so tight, but managed to ride the inch of his shaft until she was able to take more. With the feeling, and the sights, and the sounds and taste, he thought he must have died and gone to heaven. He was zeroing in on the pussy on his face, when a gentle hand took his and directed it to a very wet pussy. So with one pumping his cock, one on his mouth, and one on his hand, he wondered what the other one was going to do. He didn't have to wait long to find out. He felt a hand massaging his sweat-covered nuts. His juice exploded inside Lavish just as he hit bottom. About the same time, Lavish's cunt let loose with a stream of cum on his cock. After they untangled, Barbie was still yearning to come, so she assumed Cash's position on the table, and Lesa licked her pussy while Dria set on her face. Cash and Lavish watched the show before them, and it wasn't long before his rod was poking out in front of him again. He walked up behind Lesa and played with her pussy while she was still slurping Barbie. He rubbed his dick against her, and she turned around and said, "It's too big, I can't take it." He grabbed her and lifted her on the table.

"It a feel good Ma, just try it," he said kissing her and inserting his huge dick into her. She sucked on his lip as he took her breath away. She held on to him.

"Oh god yes! Fuck me!" she screamed. Cash pushed the rest of his dick into her wet pussy. Lesa was enjoying his big cock. It felt like it was precisely what she needed all these years. She was so turned on that night, she ended up fucking him for an hour straight as everybody watched. After all the sex, Cash made up his mind. He wanted them in his life, as long as they were a team. After sex they laid in Dria's bed.

"Any of y'all got a man?" Cash asked. They looked at him crazy.

"Why you asking them that?" Dria asked.

"Cuz I wanna be able to see y'all when I want, that's why."

"Nah," they all said together wondering where all this was coming from. Cash stood up and took a key off his key chain and handed it to Dria.

"What's this?" she asked looking at the key.

"The key to one of my houses, I want y'all to move in."

"Stop playing, Boy!" she said stunned.

"I ain't playing. Dria, you been riding with me for a year, so you know I don't play games," he said going in the bathroom to wash off. He wasn't in love, but finding four bad bitches with good pussy was like finding a unicorn. When Cash hopped in his car, his phone vibrated in his pocket. He pulled it out and noticed the number was blocked.

"Who the fuck is this?" he asked standoffish.

"This Big G," a deep voice said. Cash smiled. Just like he had expected – Big G was ready to talk business. He knew his money wasn't long enough to go to war with him.

"Fuck you want, Nigga," Cash said, standing on him a little bit.

"I wanna talk business," Big G said in a defeated voice.

"I know it, I know it," Cash yelled smiling. Deep down inside he was ready to end the war as well.

Chapter 13

JUNE

June left the meeting feeling exploited; he knew what Cash was doing. He wanted him busy to make sure he knew his whereabouts. One good thing did come outta this – the spot on the block was legitimate now, but this definitely made his plan harder in Beloit. He thought of a way around it. There was only two niggas to decimate, and he would use Kim to kill two birds with one stone. He dropped the bricks off at the spot and the money at his mom's house. She didn't ask questions about where he got it. He told her $100,000 was for a down payment on a house. She was delighted, and it made him feel good being able to move his mom out the hood. It was a dream come true for a young hustler. He picked Kim up after dropping off the money, and told her the plan. She was down like always. He was going to keep her around. They didn't have long to make it happen. He needed to be back in the morning to set up shop.

(AN HOUR LATER IN THE B)

"Thank you for coming, Cam," Kim cried. "It ain't shit, Girl. Stop crying," he tried to reassure her.

"I know me and him didn't always get along, but I can't believe he gone," she yelled, laying it on thick. She played the role of a grieving baby momma to a tee.

"Calm down, Ma, we gone find out who did this and lay them down," he said, taking a seat.

"I know it's just hard living without him," she said.

"Come here, Ma," he said, holding his arm out to give her a hug. Kim made sure to press against him to see if he was strapped, and he was. She stared into his eyes and saw lust. He had always wanted her, but she wasn't attracted to his fat ass. He leaned in to kiss her and she met him halfway. He grabbed her fat ass as she took off his shirt removing his gun and putting it outta reach. She broke the kiss when June came up behind him, putting his 40 to his dome.

"Don't move, Pussy," he said.

"What the fuck is this, Kim?" Cam asked shocked.

"What the fuck it look like, Nigga?" she asked, picking up his gun and putting it to his face.

"What's this about, money?" Cam asked, too laid back for June's taste so he slapped him upside the head with the hammer, knocking him to the floor.

"Don't say shit else unless I say so," June said.

"Aight, you got…" he started, but June hit him again, cutting him off.

"What the fuck I tell you, Nigga?" This time he didn't say anything. June got the tape and taped him to a chair.

"Now I'm gone ask you this once. Where the coke and the money at?" June asked placing a rug on the floor and then flipping the chair over on it.

"My wife got the money and my mans' got the bricks, you ain't gotta kill me," he begged for his life.

"Kim, I thought you said he was a real nigga?" June asked laughing.

"Bae, I guess I didn't know any better until I met you," she replied in a sexy tone, giving him a kiss.

"Call your wife. Tell her to bring all your cash now because you gotta bust a move," June instructed him going in his pants and getting his phone.

"What's her number?"

"It's under 'wifey'," he said. June found the number and made the call. He placed the phone on speaker. It rang two times before a female voice said "hello."

"Yo, I'm.... Imma need you to bring all my cash to Kim crib, I gotta bust this move real quick," he said embarrassed.

"What move you gotta bust?" she asked, being nosy.

"Look, Bitch, stop questioning me and do what I said." June hung the phone up right away without letting her respond.

"That bitch better show up or you dead," June said.

"She a be here, bro, you ain't gotta kill me." June looked at him crying like a lil bitch, but once he got the money all they ass was dead.

"Call your mans with the bricks and tell him the same thing." He called and did exactly what he was told. Now all they had to do was wait.

Twenty minutes after they made the call, his wife knocked on the door with two big duffle bags in her hand. Kim let her in while June waited behind the door. She came in talking shit.

"Kim, if you and Cam'ron fucking, I'm gone beat yo ass," she said walking into the house. She instantly stopped once she saw her man taped up.

"What the fuck," was all she got out before June bashed her in the head with the massive handgun, knocking her out cold.

"That bitch talk too much," he said.

"Yeah, I never liked her ass either," Kim said kicking her before getting the tape to tie her up. As soon as she was done, there was another knock at the door. Kim opened it again.

"When you and Cam'ron start fucking?" Dude asked. When he walked inside, he tried grabbing his strap once he saw his mans and his wife tied up.

"Do it, bitch ass nigga, and Imma dome yo ass," June said with his 40 pointed at the back of his head. He put his hands up, dropping his bag. Kim took his gun off him and taped him up as well.

(JUNE)

June and Kim sat at the table counting the money they took from Cam'ron. It was over half a mil and three bricks. This was the lick of a lifetime, and it came right on time. They waited until nightfall to load them into a stolen car outside. He told Kim to follow him in his car to a block in Janesville where he killed the two men, and gave Kim the command to take care of the wife. She had no problem pulling the trigger, and June knew she was the one he'd been searching for. They made it back to Chicago before the morning, and June set up shop. Kim went back to Beloit to help Fat Boy. He sent the three bricks to Fat Boy, and took the money to his mom's before getting a hotel and going to sleep. He dreamed about the $700,000 he made in less than a week. Life was good and all he needed to become king was to take care of Cash.

(KIA – A WEEK LATER)

The last week was delightful. She enjoyed hanging with her girls. She missed them already as she headed home. She stayed as long as possible, waiting on her face to heal. She couldn't wait to see Angel and Money. There was nothing like the love she felt around them. Not even the power trip she'd been on lately. The short time she spent away from them showed her how much she was in love. She never thought she would have feelings for a man, but Money broke the icebox where her heart used to be. She couldn't help letting him in. She loved the way he walked, and the way he looked when he was sleeping. She thought about it as she rode home lip singing to Keisha Cole. "*Love, never knew what I was missing, but I knew once we start kissing, I found love.*" She couldn't help laughing at herself; she had it bad. She wasn't the type to listen to slow jams, but Angel and Money definitely had her feeling some type of way. She pulled up to the house and parked her car. Inside her bag was 200 bandz from the work. Their spot was booming out of this world. Her life was changing by the minute - she found love and more money then she knew what to do with. She unlocked the door, and Angel was standing there with a big smile on her face. She was wearing boy shorts as usual and looked good enough to eat.

"Hey Girl," she said giving Angel a hug and kiss. The connection between them was amazing.

"Where Money?" Kia asked.

"He still in the bed. I put his ass to sleep last night with this good pussy," Angel said and they laughed.

"What's in the bag, Bitch? You better not went shopping without me," Angel said with her face screwed up.

"Now you know a bitch ain't played you like that, this the money I made this week outta town," she said going to sit in the living room to recount the money. She wanted it to be correct before she gave it to Money. Even though she was getting over on the price of the bricks, she still wanted his trust. Angel came over taking the money from her.

"Let me find out you starting to act like Money, Bitch, with this business first shit," she said with a smile on her face.

"Bitch, quit playing, you know I gotta make sure this money right for Daddy."

"Well, what about making sure I'm good," Angel said pouring the money on the floor. Kia laughed inside because Angel was crazy. Angel started to undress. It didn't take long before she was ass naked standing right in front of Kia, the way she stood there was so sexy. She had a body of a goddess. She laid on top of the money and played with her clit. Kia felt her pussy become moist from watching her please herself.

"Oh shit, Kia, I missed you, did you miss Mommy?" she asked licking her fingers putting them inside her walls and using the other hand to play with her clit.

"Ya I missed you, Baby," Kia replied in a sexy tone, dropping between Angel legs. They begin to kiss long and hard. Kia removed Angels fingers from her pussy and inserted her fingers in to her mouth, sucking on them.

"You like that taste, Baby?" Angel asked, outta breath.

"I love the taste of your pussy," she said before going down on her.

(MEANWHILE – 10:00 A.M., MONEY)

Money woke up to the sound of loud moans coming from downstairs. He hopped outta bed and walked halfway down the steps, and what he saw turned his morning hard on larger. Not wanting to miss out on the action, he instantly rushed to the bathroom and brushed his teeth before he headed downstairs. His women were in a 69 position eating each other out like it was the last meal they'd ever have. They were moaning so loud that they didn't even notice his entrance.

"I see y'all having breakfast without me," he said with a smirk on his face. They looked up.

"We not finished with breakfast, we waiting on the sausage," Kia said. Money walked over and bent down and put his dick in her mouth. She begin to alternate between swirling her tongue around the head and sucking up and down on his shaft. A quiver passed through her body, and she moaned with excitement around his cock. All this time Angel was licking Kia's pussy. Money begin to fuck Kia's face holding on to her head. He stopped before he nutted because he was just getting started. He instructed Kia to eat Angel's pussy as he got behind her and started eating her ass.

"Ooohhhh shit, that feels good," Kia moaned.

"You like that?" he asked, sticking his tongue in her ass. She gasped in delight as she came.

"I'm cumming," Angel yelled out before cumming all over Kia's face. Kia continued to lick up all of her juices. Money demanded they get on their hands and knees side by side. He got behind Angel and entered her already wet pussy from the back. He thrust in and out of her. Kia and Angel shared a kiss at the same time. The flow of her juices told him she was really enjoying herself. She begin to throw that ass back. He switched over to Kia as Angel played with her pussy. For 20 minutes he switched between them before he pulled out and nutted all over their faces, feeling like a boss nigga.

(CHICAGO)

Just as they expected, June was plotting. A week ago he hit them with five birds. He told them Cash gave him the green light for the spot, so they could turn it up to the next level. The last few weeks, they been making nine bands a day. The war with the G-boys had ended so they were free to move as they pleased. They were up the block with a few of the guys. Everyone was still strapped, even though Cash trusted Big G's word, they didn't. They lost too many homies to ever trust that nigga, and if any of them ever saw him, it was a flat line, no questions asked.

"It feels good to stand on the block without having to worry about them G-boys coming through," Tre Boi said with a cup of lean in his hand.

"It do on the low, but think about how many niggas can't say that," Ryan said pouring out some drink for the dead homies.

"R.I.P. to the guys," he said and a tear fell from his eyes thinking about Blue. He reminisced about the time Blue saved his life. He wiped the tear away, and nobody said anything because they felt the same way at one time or another.

"Ya, R.I.P. to the guys," TDN said shaking his head. It was silent for a few moments as they thought about all the faces they would never see again. But that was life in the city, kill or be killed.

TDN opened up his car door and played Future "Deeper Than The Ocean."

I put spikes around my jacket and I'm strapped up with that ratchet, I'm chasing after paper and I became a savage, a nigga set my nigga up the game is full of madness, sometimes I wanna get inside the escalade and crash it. My pain running deeper than the ocean.

"That's my shit, Bro," Tre Boi said, reaching his hand out to shake up with Ryan as the music kept playing.

"On Dave, he got off on that shit," Ryan said breaking the handshake. The blue Cadillac the G-boys was known to be in came up the block and everybody pulled their strap out just in case. But the car kept it moving.

"Damn, we should've lit that bitch up," TDN said.

"Then we would be right back at war. Big G sent them through to see what would happen," Tre Boi said putting his 9 back under his hoodie.

"Ya, you right, then the nigga Cash would be gunning for us," Ryan said and everyone agreed. It was insane how everybody knew he was a snake, but nobody did anything about it. Ryan hoped June murked him when it was all said and done. He wondered how many of the other guys felt the same.

Chapter 14

KIA, A WEEK LATER

*K*ia left from her gun class. After getting kidnapped by Dajunema, she wanted to learn to protect herself and get her concealed carrier. She felt something was wrong last week. Money got dressed and left the house with a gun under his hoodie. When they first started doing business, he didn't carry a firearm. She wanted to protect herself just in case.

After leaving her class, she called her girl Tay to check on business.

"We should be done with all three bricks in a week," Tay told her. Things had picked up from when she and Money left, and it took them a month to get to that point. It only took her girls two weeks. She believed they would turn up, but not like this, they really impressed her. They would have to upgrade to six bricks a month making $1.4 million a month in profit, and 100 Gs she'd save for taxing Money. She called Angel to see what she was doing at the club. Angel spent most of her time at the club working, even when they were rich. When the money came back from this move, they would be worth a million in cash. Sometimes she didn't understand her.

"What the fuck you want?" Angel asked, pretending to be upset.

"Girl, what the fuck you mad about?" Kia asked.

"Bitch, I'm just playing. You call yourself my best friend and fell for that shit," she said laughing.

"Bitch, you know you the queen of faking. You spent all those years faking orgasms having phone sex while Money was in prison." They laughed.

"What the fuck you want Bitch cause I'm working?"

"I wanted to see what you doing," Kia said.

"You really want to know?"

"Yeah or I wouldn't asked."

"I ain't doing shit, sitting in my office having a drink and watching everybody else work."

"You drinking, at this time of day?" Kia asked, frowning.

"Yeah, I ain't got shit better to do. Why, what you doing?"

"Shit, I wanna know if you wanna go shopping," Kia said knowing she wouldn't turn down a chance to shop.

"Bitch, why you ask something like that, shopping is my middle name."

"Well, I'm pulling up outside, bring yo ass on."

"Imma be out in five minutes," she said hanging up in Kia's face. Kia sat in the car playing music, moving her body like a snake to the beat. She felt like she was on top of the world. With money, power, and respect, she felt like a god. The more money she made, the more authority she wanted. It was like a drug to a girl who never had shit.

(MEANWHILE - BELOIT, RE RE)

Re Re pulled up to the house after going to the Western Union to pick up two bands Money sent her. Normally she would be delighted to receive the money, but it felt bitter sweet this time. She wished he'd spend time with her, but he stay with his girls. She turned off the engine stepping outta the car. The wind blew her hair every way possible as she went in the house. There wasn't a soul there, Lo Lo and her sister went outta town. She took a shower before laying in bed, miserable. It was funny how fast life changed, she was accustomed to being the player and now she was being played. How could she allow herself to fall for him. She wondered was it the sex or just his swag? Was it the fact he wasn't hers and didn't wanna be? She felt like her heart was ambushed, and she was surprised to find herself in love. She picked up her cell phone and texted him.

"When Imma see you again?" He responded right back.

"Soon, did you get that cash?"

"Ya, but it's not money I want."

"Come on Re Re, we talked about this already and you got mad. I thought we had an understanding." Seeing his response was heart breaking and she felt inconsolable. He was right, he wasn't her man, he told her everything from the beginning. She had to accept his relationship, even if she hated to.

"Ya, you're right, I'm sorry. I just miss you," she confessed.

"I miss you too Ma, just work with me. You should know I wanna see you too."

She laid her head on her pillow and took a deep breath. The insecure girl in her wanted to question him about having feelings for her, but the woman in her would relax and chill. She texted him back.

"Ok, I'm with you no matter what."

"That's what I needed to hear," he responded back.

"Just text me when you wanna see me."

"Cool, I gotta go. I think somebody following me." Re Re sat up in bed and said a prayer, hoping everything was ok.

(MEANWHILE – KILLA)

Killa tailed Money from his house. He found out where he lived last night after following Angel home from the club. He needed to murder Money for trying to slay him. He didn't tell his brother because he would've acted on impulse and gotten them killed. Even though Cash didn't fuck with his brother, he made it clear when June pulled a gun on him that nobody was to harm his family. Killa wasn't gone let him get away with shooting him. Money signed his death certificate that night.

"Don't get too close up on him," Killa told his mans Mook. He didn't wanna be noticed. He checked the chamber on the AK47 on his lap. He had two clips taped together just in case things didn't go as planed. Money stopped at the light.

"Yo, pull on the driver side," Killa instructed. When he tried to, Money cut them off. What he did next caught him off guard. He hopped out, letting off rounds. Boc! Boc! Boc! Boc! Boc! Boc!

Mook got hit in the head with one of the shots, killing him on impact. Killa pulled the AK up and fired back without aiming. Money backed up and ran behind his car giving Killa time to step outta his automobile clutching the AK in his left hand. He started his counter attack letting off 20 rounds, most of them slamming into the car, shattering the window, and broken glass rained down on Money. Still determined to get his target, Killa advanced on the Bentley. Money stood over the roof and fired BOC!BOC!BOC! Killa ducked down. He heard the bullets rip passed his head. He heard sirens and knew it wouldn't be long before the police came. He ran back to his car and pulled Mook's dead body out and jumped in. As he left, he saw Money get in his car and pull off. He wanted to go after him for his dead homie, but their war was only beginning. He gave it to Money; he wasn't a bitch like he first thought.

(MONEY)

Money pulled up to the house and parked before hopping out looking at the damage. His car was demolished, but he was alive. He noticed he was being followed about 20 minutes after leaving the house, so they knew where he laid his head. When he saw Killa, he understood shit was real. He can't believe they tried to pull that stunt. When they attempted to pull up on the side of him, he was prepared and made his move. They must have thought he was stupid. He shocked them when he jumped out letting off. Yeah, they weren't qualified for war with a killa like him. He could still envision the bullet going through the driver's fitted cap, pushing his shit in. He needed to do something with his car ASAP. He pulled it all the way up the driveway getting it off the street. Just as he parked, Angel and Kia pulled up behind him.

"What the fuck happened to yo car?" Angel asked, walking over to him.

"Some muthafucka tried getting down on me."

"What! Who Baby?" Kia asked, coming over giving him a hug. Angel stood there with a frightened expression on her face.

"What the fuck is going on, Money? What happened? Who you get into it with?" Angel asked question after question.

"Look, we ain't got time for that right now. Kia, do you know somebody that could fix this car with no questions asked?"

"Ya."

"Ok, then Imma need you to call them now. Tell them to get here ASAP. Let them know money isn't a problem. Angel, stop standing there looking stupid and go get the money out the house, and put it in Kia's car. We gotta move."

"Move for what?" she asked.

"Just do what the fuck I said!" he yelled.

"Whatever," she replied, walking off rolling her eyes at him. Kia was on the phone doing as he asked. It was best to get outta this house, he wasn't about to chance it and stay there. He believed they followed him from there. He ran inside to help Angel get the money. When he walked in the room, she was throwing money in a bag and crying. He came up behind her and hugged her.

"I'm sorry, Ma. I didn't mean to talk to you like that; it's just they tried to kill me today. Bae, I'm just worried they might try to hurt y'all. It's my job to protect y'all and I need you to trust me on this," he said kissing the back of her neck. She rotated staring deep into his eyes, and he saw the hurt plastered across her face.

"This is why I didn't want you back in the game," she said through tears. Kia was standing in the doorway.

"He's sending someone over now. We could leave and put the keys in yo car, but it's up to you baby."

"Come on, let's go, we staying in a hotel tonight. In the morning I want you to find us a new house," he said talking to Angel. They each grabbed a duffle bag full of money and left. Money thought to himself, *Imma have to find that lil nigga and murk him right away.* He wasn't with this hiding shit. When they arrived at the Trump International Hotel in downtown Chicago, Angel checked them into a room before falling asleep. Money saw she was worried sick. He took a pre-rolled blunt out and Kia put a towel under the door to stop the smoke from leaving their room.

"Can I ask you something, Money?"

"Ya, anything," he said, hitting the blunt two times.

"Are you a boss nigga?"

"What?"

"I said, are you a boss nigga?" she repeated.

"Ya, what made you ask that?" he questioned.

"Cause what happened today wasn't a boss move, baby."

"What the fuck you mean?" he asked offended by the way she was coming at him.

"Just listen before you get in yo chest. Cause what I'm about to tell you comes from the heart. A boss nigga has hitters, and he not in the streets having shootouts in the middle of the day. We are about to be millionaires and your raising all this over what?" she asked coming over sitting on his lap.

"Respect, niggas gone respect me in these streets," he said taking another pull off the blunt.

"So you going put in yo own work?"

"Hell ya, I gotta get this lil nigga." She kissed him on the lips.

"Daddy, sit back and watch how yo bitch get down."

"Nah, I don't want you in this shit. I got it," he said, meaning every word. He wasn't try'na see anything happen to his girls, he would give his life before he let that happen.

"Come on, Daddy, I won't even have to leave this room to get it done, and Angel won't have to move outta her house. You know she love that crib," she said smiling.

"You want have to leave this room?" he asked, raising his eyebrows.

"Not at all. All I need is a name."

"Show Daddy something then," he said kissing her.

(MEANWHILE – KILLA)

Killa arrived in Chicago an hour ago. He was furious about loosing Mook, and didn't know how to explain his murder to the team. Cash would demand answers and want the head of the person responsible. Killa needed time to clear his mind to get his story together, so he went to his mom's house to relax. She was asleep. Killa closed his room door, set his AK under the bed and flamed up a blunt. He fucked up going after Money without Cash's approval. But he couldn't let Money get away with disrespecting him. Thoughts of confessing to June crossed his mind, but he dismissed them. He was a man and could stand on his own two feet, he didn't need June to bail him out. He smoked some weed before going to sleep.

(KIA)

Kia acted like she needed to pee and once inside the bathroom she called Dajunema.

"Hi, Kia," he said answering the phone.

"Hey, I know you said things between us are just business now, but I really need your help with something," she cried.

"What is the problem? Because I'll take care of it," he asked heatedly.

"There is this dude outta Chicago named Killa, he tried to rape me."

"He did what?" Danjunema yelled.

"He tried to rape me," she said.

"That nigga is dead, you don't have to worry anymore. Baby girl, I will take care of it. All I need is a picture of the bitch ass nigga. Do you have any info on this son of a bitch?" he asked in a thick accent.

"All I have is pictures off his Instagram," she said outta breath from the performance she was putting on.

"That's all I need, stop crying, it's taken care of."

"Ok thanks," she said hanging the phone up. She wiped away her fake tears and went back in the room with Money.

"What, you took a shit?" he asked, smiling.

"Nah, I was on Facebook, crazy ass boy," she said bending down in between his legs to give him head. The newfound dominance she had really turned her on. The day Dajunema took her hostage showed her he was a powerful man. The fact that he was in love with her meant she could manipulate him into doing her dirty work. She took Money's dick into her mouth sucking on the head.

"Ya, just like that, Ma." She pulled him out her mouth looking at his sexy cock. Pre-cum was oozing out the head. Money smiled and put his hand on the back of her head making her swallow him whole. She loved that shit. He was the only man she would let control her, and she would do anything to protect him and Angel, even play games with the devil.

(MEANWHILE – DANJUNEMA)

Danjunema called Chipo and put the hit out on Killa. It didn't take long for him to discover he lived on 24th and Normal Avenue. He sent Gero and Chipo to assassinate him, but gave strict instructions not to murder any women or children. He was old school and against killing adolescents. Kia getting raped was the reason he insisted on her being with him. He gave her freedom and look where it got them. He was running out of options to get her devotion. He wouldn't be able to live with himself if something happen to her, and he was willing to do anything to protect her. Killa would be a sacrifice to show his love to the only woman he couldn't possess. Taking a sip from his drink, he thought it might bring her running to him for safety.

Chapter 15

MONEY, 5-8-2016, 8:00 A.M., THE NEXT DAY

"Money, wake up, look what happened," Kia said pointing to the T.V. The news was on. The police found a body hanging from a streetlight, decapitated.

"Who the fuck is that?" he asked.

"That was our problem, now we can go home," she said giving him a kiss on the lips. She shook Angel telling her too. "We're getting ready to go home."

"What?" she asked still half asleep.

"I said get up, we getting ready to go home, I'm about to take a shower, you want to join?" Kia asked walking into the bathroom and turning on the shower. Without closing the door, she got naked and stepped in.

"Baby, what is she talking about?" Angel said sitting up in bed. Money couldn't believe his eyes. A picture of Killa was on the news, they confirmed he'd been killed last night.

"Money, I know you hear me," Angel asked.

"What you say?"

"I said, what is she talking about we going home? What happened?"

"I don't know Ma, but everything is ok, and we going back to the crib." Last night he thought about Killa coming after him, and he wondered if Cash had sent him, but it didn't take much thought. His brother would never take their beef that far.

"That's good because I didn't want to move," she said sincerely. Money was lost. What the fuck did Kia do? And how? The shit on the news was really fucked up. The person responsible for this was an animal. He knew there was more to Kia than she let on. She tried to play that nice role, but in order to get something like this done, she was connected with some powerful muthafuckas. He just wondered who.

(MEANWHILE – JUNE)

June and Kim were asleep in a hotel in Downtown Chicago. June's phone was ringing non-stop for the last 30 minutes. He didn't want to get up and grab it outta his pants, laying on the floor. Whoever was calling was set on getting through, so he hopped outta bed half asleep to answer. He picked up and saw his mom's number.

"What up, Ma," he said wondering why she was calling.

"They killed my baby!" she yelled in the phone, crying hysterically. He couldn't understand what she was saying.

"What happened, Ma?"

"They killed my son," she cried.

"Ma, Imma need you to stop crying and tell me what happened. Cause I can't understand what your saying."

She calmed down a little before saying, "They came into my house last night Baby, and took your brother and beat and killed him right in front of me," she yelled crying harder. "They cut my baby head off like he was an animal."

June broke down crying. Who would do something like this to his little brother? He heard his mom crying on the line. "I'm on my way home Ma, whoever did this gone pay," he cried without shame.

"Bae, is everything ok?" Kim asked sitting up in bed. He wiped away his tears.

"I'm on my way to come get you now. Don't worry, I'm not gone let nothing happen to you," he stated before hanging up the line. He began to get dressed.

"Is everything alright?" Kim asked again as she got outta bed to get dressed.

"Nah, somebody killed my little brother," he said breaking down.

"I'm so sorry, Baby," she said hugging him as he cried. "You gotta be strong for your mom, ok Daddy, stop crying," she said lifting his head up staring in his eyes. "We gotta make them pay for every tear you shed. I need you to get your head together so we can do that, ok Daddy?"

Seeing the cold look in her eyes made him feel prepared to avenge his brother. She wiped his tears away and kissed him on the forehead. "You ready?" she asked him.

"Ya."

"Then let's go."

He tucked his 9MM in his pocket and they left the hotel. When they made it downstairs, he saw Cash's brother with two of the baddest bitches he ever seen getting inside a car. He thought about the night he put his hands on him and wanted to murder him, but he had other things to take care.

June pulled up to the spot with tears in his eyes, a mac 11 with two clips taped together, on a shoestring hanging around his neck. Kim was strapped with two 9s with 30 clips, braced for war. Ten minutes after his mom called, he called a meeting with what was left over of his team. Everyone was standing around with hoodies on, strapped and ready for his orders. A few of them held in their tears, the only thing they wanted to shed was blood for their lost brother.

"So, what's the word on the street?" June asked walking to the middle of the room. "I wanna know something. I need to know something," he yelled taking a bottle of Hennessey from Tre Boi. He turned it upside down, hoping to wash the pain away. The room was quieter then a cemetery at 3 a.m. The streets wasn't talking, and nobody knew what happened to Killa. June smashed the bottle.

"What the fuck everybody looking stupid for, tell me something!" he said with pleading eyes. The tears that were being held back fell free at the sight of their leader breaking down. They were ready to declare war but with who?

Chapter 16

5-15-16, A WEEK LATER IN BELOIT

The sun was shining bright without a cloud in the sky. Temperatures were in the middle 60s when Money jumped on I-90 to visit Re Re. His thoughts were on getting some of that good head and informing her that as long as she played her part, she could remain in his life. Over the last few months, he developed feelings for her. He couldn't explain them. It wasn't love, he understood that, and it wasn't just lust. He respected her despite how they met, and if he wasn't in a relationship, he'd be with her. He parked outside Lo Lo's house and went to the door. Re Re opened it looking amazing. He hair was pulled back and she was wearing a light blue Gucci bodycon dress with the matching shoes. Her skin was oiled down and something in his heart felt like they had a chance at something great. She smoothed her dress out as he looked her over.

"You like?" she asked, stepping aside to allow him to enter.

"Ya, you look good, Ma," he said, giving her a hug.

"So where we going?" he asked Re Re as she turned around, wrapping her arms around his neck and staring into his eyes.

"I'm not try'na go anywhere," she said dropping to her knees rubbing his cock through his jeans.

"You crazy, Ma, I'm try'na take you out," he said smiling.

"I'm trying to do the same," she replied unbuttoning his pants.

"Where Lo and them at?" Money asked not wanting to disrespect his crib.

"Outta town," Re said putting his dick into her mouth and sucking on the head before pulling it out and licking him from the sack up. He leaned back against the wall enjoying the pleasure. She spit on his tool and jacked him using both hands, staring in his eyes.

"You like it when I spit on yo dick?" she asked still pulling on him. His eyes were closed.

"Suck it for me, Ma," She took it in her mouth and deep throated him, her nose was in his pubic hairs. She pulled it out and went all the way down again. Re Re wasn't a fool, she wanted him and she thought the best way was sucking him up. She pulled him out her mouth.

"Fuck my face, push that cock down my throat." Money didn't respond. He grabbed her hair and slowly push himself down her throat. He went at it like this for 15 minutes before pulling out and cumming on her face. Re Re got up and went to take a shower, Money pulled up his Trues and walked back to her room. It was crazy how she could make his heart melt with head. He felt horrible for cheating, but wasn't ready to stop even if that meant betraying the love of his life. Money undressed and went to take a shower with his gutta bitch. After another round of sex, they settled on her bed.

"Ma, I want you to look for your own spot," Money said playing in her hair.

"Ya," she said still rubbing his chest. She couldn't get enough of him. He had swag but it was the cock she was after.

"Ya, I'mma give you cash and pay the rent, how that sound?"

"It's cool, but is you gone come through more? I'm not try'na be alone all the time."

Money kissed her forehead. "Ya, I can do that." Re Re's heart skipped a beat. She wondered if there was a chance as she lay in his arms.

(JUNE, 5-29-2016, TWO WEEKS LATER)

After his brother's funeral two weeks ago, June was finding it really hard to find leads on who killed his blood, and it was driving him insane. At the funeral everybody came to show their respects to his family. Cash wouldn't take no for an answer when he offered to pay for everything. His brother went out in style like a true D-boy. At the repass Chief Keef performed "Don't Like." That was Killa's theme song even though the song was old. He used to play it like it just dropped. June sat inside his brother's room at his mom's old crib. He moved her out the hood ASAP after they ran in her spot. He thanked God they didn't hurt her. In his hand he held Killa's phone, but couldn't bring himself to open it, so he cut the power off before heading out. This would be his last time on the block and he wasn't gone miss it. Kim sat outside in her new 2016 Lexus RX waiting for him to come out. His life was changing for the better. He'd pulled off his plans in Beloit and Cash was now fronting Fat Boy bricks. They split the profit 60/40 his way so he was bringing in $100,000 every two weeks off that alone. Not to mention the block he ran for Cash, and the $500,000 he had saved. He was upset he wasn't there when his brother died. He thought he could've saved him. He opened the passenger door and hopped in, leaned the seat back, and lit up a blunt.

"You ok?" Kim asked, looking over at him. She had a sad expression on her face. Seeing him grieving hurt her. Over the time they spent together, they became close. He planned on making her his girl, she proved her worth a while ago. All she wanted was somebody to love her, and keep it real. He could give her that and so much more.

"I'm good, Baby," he said taking a pull from his blunt and blowing out the smoke.

"Where we headed, Daddy?" she asked putting her hand on his lap.

"I don't know, wherever you wanna go cool with me," he said thanking God for loud because if it wasn't for smoking, he might lose his mind. It kept him cool and calm, stopping him from pushing a nigga's shit back for kicks. Half the time he wanted to kill Cash. He felt what ever happened to his brother had something to do with him. He didn't believe Cash wanted him murdered, but whoever did more than likely wanted Cash dead as well. Only thing stopping him was the fact his lil bro loved him like a blood brother. Killa would've given his life to protect him. His thoughts about his brother brought tears to his eyes. Damn, why the good die young?

(CHICAGO)

Tre Boi drove the city streets in his new 2017 Audi AS coupe. Behind him was a 2017 A3, A5, and Audi 6. Just as June expected, Tre Boi and Big Ryan were excellent hustlers. They showed loyalty every day. The money was never short, and June left them to be their own bosses. They didn't have to worry about him standing over them watching their every move. It was crazy how everything changed so fast. They couldn't believe how much they elevated their hustle. They pulled over, and Tre Boi hopped out wearing Louis Vuitton from head to toe. He walked over to Big Ryan, smoking a blunt. Ryan sat behind the wheel of his Audi A5, Gucci down.

"Fuck you pull over for?" Ryan yelled over his new mix tape.

"Man, turn that bullshit down," Tre Boi joked with his mans. Ryan was hot with them bars, but he was knee deep in the streets. He was seeing more money than most rappers, selling coke.

"On what, my nigga hating?" Ryan laughed cutting the music down.

"Nah, Broski, I'm just fucking withchu," he said putting his head in the window.

"Fuck you stop for then," Ryan said passing his female passenger a blunt to roll up.

"I need some more ice for my drink."

"Shit, me too," Ryan said looking in his cup. "Ay Lil Mama, when you get done rolling that blunt, hop in the driver's seat" he added, getting out and going in the store with Tre Boi.

"Ah, B, what that little bitch on?" Tre Boi asked going to get a cup to fill it up with ice.

"Shit, Skud really. She got some good head, pussy aight."

"It's just aight, Skud?" Tre Boi asked unable to believe a bitch that bad had pussy that was weak.

"It's cool, Bro, it ain't shit to write home about," he said, paying for the ice and a box of blunts. Just then, a man walked in singing Lil Jo Jo BDK, "Niggas claim 300, but we BDK." Out the corner of his eye, Ryan watched Tre Boi snake him with a left hook, knocking him out cold. He was asleep in the air before hitting the ground, which woke him back up. What they didn't know was that he was battle tested, and it only took a second to grab his 40 off his hip. They both took off out of the store as the man tried getting to his feet. They both made a mistake by leaving their pistols in the car. He chased them out, firing.

Boc!Boc!Boc!Boc!Boc!

They ran passed their cars, and he was right behind them. TDN stepped out, chasing the shooter. He wasn't gone lose another one of his homies. Ryan heard the bullets flying passed his head. TDN stopped and aimed-Boc!Boc!Boc!Boc!Boc!Boc!

The shooter fell to the floor and TDN jogged over, stood over him, and pumped him with bullets. Then he tucked his gun and ran back to his car pulling off. Ryan felt something wet running down his leg and saw he was hit.

"You good?" Tre Boi asked.

"I'm hit, B," Ryan said, limping back to his car. He hopped in the passenger side and they pulled off. Tre Boi pulled off, thinking about how close he came to losing his life. He thought about how his money was long now, he couldn't afford to be in trouble. They accomplished so much, he wasn't trying to see it crumble.

(MEANWHILE – CASH)

The summer was almost here; it was warmer and more humid today than Cash ever remembered in May. The temperature was in the 70s. Cash sat in the back of his Bentley Bentayga as his driver took him to pick up this bitch he met the other night. He no longer drove around with his hitters. After what happened to Killa, he didn't feel safe, so he hired a security team of ex-marines. He wasn't a hoe by any means and put in his own work if necessary, but who ever killed Killa was a sick muthafucker. When they found his head, they found his dick in his mouth with the words "cock sucker" printed on his forehead. All the Hennessy in the world couldn't take his mind off his lil nigga. He drank cup after cup in memory of his fallen soldier. Somebody would pay for this, but who? The streets weren't talking, nobody knew anything and that's what scared him most. He picked his phone up and dialed his lil move number.

"I'm pulling up. Come outside," he said and hung up. When they arrived, she was standing on the sidewalk waiting. She was sexy as hell; he wasn't going to lie. She reminded him of the model Ms. Cat and was stacked like her too with 34DD-25-42. She had on a pair of True Religion jeans and looked thick. Those jeans did her justice. His driver got out and opened the door for her. She hopped in and thanked him as he closed it.

"You looking nice," he said, sipping on his drink.

"You don't look bad yo self," she said.

"I never look bad, Ma, that's what money do," he said, glancing at her.

"I'm feeling that," she said, licking her lips seductively.

"You ain't the only one Ma, but what you try'na get into?" he asked in a disengaged tone. He had a problem with commitment. A woman couldn't hold his heart. He only used them, most times keeping them around a few months before leaving without a reason.

"I don't know, it's up to you, I'm on yo time, handsome," she said leaning back in her seat.

"Ok, then Imma need you to take care of something for me," he said pulling his dick out. It stood at attention.

"Oh my god," she said, shocked, but it didn't stop her from reaching for it.

"It's so big," she said taking it in her hand. He didn't have the longest dick, it was 7 inches, but it was extremely thick, as big as her forearm.

"Suck it, bitches tell me it taste as good as it feels." With that she guided her head down to his fat cock stretching her mouth wide as she could to fit all 7 inches down her throat, but only got 3 or 4 inches down. He started to push her head further down onto his cock, but there was no way she could fit more. It didn't stop her from trying.

"Ay, white boy Rob, pull downtown I want to take her shopping," he said as he continued to fuck her face. By the time they made it downtown, he was nutting in her mouth, and she was careful not to get any on his Robin jeans.

(MEANWHILE – MONEY)

Money spent the day with his girls shopping. Now that he wasn't making moves, he didn't have anything to do, and missed the game. The other day Kia told him she wanted to start moving keys out in Madison. He convinced her that wasn't a good idea because people would have the same product as them, which would slow the trap down. She agreed with him and came up with a new plan to market them in Milwaukee and Green Bay. Once she broke it down to him, he was all for it. This would be his way back in the streets. Shit, all this laying around and spending money was becoming boring. Yeah, he was ready to get to work.

"Baby, I know you hear me calling yo ass," Angel said, breaking his daydream.

"What's good, Ma?"

"I said we ready to go, Boy. Where the hell did you go?"

"You in this bitch lacking, daydreaming and shit," Kia added.

"We been here four hours, I know y'all ain't expect me to stay the whole time. All y'all been doing is asking me what I like only to pick the opposite from what I told y'all." They laughed at his frustration.

"Let's get the baby home," Angel said, giving Kia a high five. Money headed for the door, holding it open for his ladies, when Cash walked in with a bad bitch.

"I know they ain't got my bro working as a doorman," Cash said and his friend laughed.

"How many times I gotta tell you, stop playing with me nigga. What you ain't learn from what happen to Killa?" Money asked, smirking.

That wiped the smile right off Cash's face. "What, you did that to Lil Homie?" Cash asked.

"Nah, I ain't say that, but people gotta be more careful cause that shit could happen to anybody," he said following his ladies out the door, leaving Cash standing there.

Once they got inside the car, Kia asked, "What the problem with you and your brother?"

He laid his legs across the back seat and started breaking down a blunt. "It's a long story that I don't feel like telling," he stated.

"Well one day I wanna know. Ok Daddy?"

"Aight, I got you." He hated fighting with Cash and wanted to talk to him. Life was too short for them to be into it with each other. But his pride wouldn't let him reach out to him first. Sometimes Cash could be an asshole. Money wanted to work things out but he didn't want him thinking he needed anything from him. So if Cash didn't come and apologize first, it wouldn't get done.

"You ok, Daddy?" Angel asked.

"Ya, I'm good Baby. I ain't letting that nigga get to me. Don't worry," he claimed.

"Just making sure," she said turning the music up. He watched her and Kia turned up and that brought a smile to his face. He was living every man's dream with money, cars, and two ride or die bitches, only problem was one didn't trust him. He confided with her about everything as far as business, but she wouldn't tell him anything about the connect, or how she pulled that shit off with Killa. He didn't want to push her, but was starting to feel played. In his heart he trusted her, but the inner hustler in him wanted to meet the connect.

Chapter 17

6-13-16, TWO WEEKS LATER, JUNE

*I*t was hot and humid. June leaned back in his Camero on 26-inch rims with Kim in the passenger side, crushing the streets of Chicago with Future pouring from the speakers. Life was decent. Everything was looking up. He only had two problems: one was finding out who killed his brother, and the other was finding a new connect. Cash was holding him back. He was young and hungry. Even though his pockets were a lot fatter, he had bigger plans. The Beloit thing had him eating good over 200 bandz a month, but that wasn't shit compared to the money he'd see with Cash out the picture. The only thing keeping Cash alive was he needed him for the product. If it wasn't for that, he would've marked him already. But he had a new plan that went into effect tonight. He was gone start hitting Cash's spots with the team of young savages he handpicked from the mud. Kutta and Bullet Row were young and hungry. They would take food off anybody's table. They just didn't give a fuck. It was kill or be killed with them. They grew up in the Gardens, the dirty 1-30. They lived wild and were monsters with gunplay. Bullet was light-skinned with neat dread-locks. Most niggas let his pretty boy smile and good looks mislead them to thinking he was sweet until he showed he was indeed a savage. He was a person who loved having fun and joking around, but when it was time to put his murder game down, he was all business. Kutta, on the other hand, was about 5'11" with a short cut and a beard, he favored NBA star James Harrden. Most of their life they were petty nickel and dime hustlers with no real success. When June presented them with an opportunity to get down with his team, they were all for it. Shit, what they had to lose? Tonight they were going to help him strip one of Cash's traps on the west side of Chicago. If everything went well, they'd be a part of the team, but for now he relaxed with his girl until nightfall. Then he'd get it the ski mask way. It was the beginning of Cash's downfall and June's come up. With a person as rich as Cash, you needed to hit him where it hurts, his pockets.

(BELOIT, LATER THAT NIGHT, RE RE)

Things were fine for Re Re. She moved into her crib and Money spent 15 bands on her furniture. He made sure to text her through-out the day and called when he was free but he still hadn't visited in a while. Re Re sat in the living room watching Braxton Family Values. She treasured the show because they reminded her of her family. Her thoughts switched to Money, and how he lied about visiting on the regular. He still hadn't seen her apartment. She didn't wanna seem ungrateful for everything he'd done for her, but she hated being alone. She used to believe money trumped love, but now she understood that once you were in love, that person is all that mattered. She stood up and walked to her room grabbing her iPhone to call Kim. She answered on the second ring.

"Hi, Boo," Kim said.

"Hey Girl, what you doing?" Re Re asked.

"At the house laying down, about to go to sleep."

"Oh! Imma let you rest," Re Re said.

"Naw, what's wrong Girl?"

"I'm not feeling this nigga try'na play me," Re Re said as tears rolled down her face. She was a mess. The world as she knew it was falling apart. Her emotions were all over, one minute she was smiling and enjoying life, the next she was crying over a man that wasn't hers.

"Girl, how he playing you? Look that nigga paying yo bills; you stay at the mall. What else you want?" Kim asked.

"I want him to spend time with me," she yelled.

"Girl, you need to pull it together before you run that nigga off. He told you from the beginning he had a woman."

"That's easy for you to say," Re Re said rolling her eyes.

"What you mean by that?" Kim asked.

"What I mean is everybody don't find Mister Right."

"Whatever Girl, June ain't Mister Right, but he good for me. Don't let me find out you hating." Kim said. Re Re knew she was wrong for what she said. Kim desired a good man after all she went through with her baby daddy.

"I'm sorry girl, I didn't mean to come for you," Re Re said apologizing.

"Don't worry about it girl, I know you ain't like that. But Imma about to come spend the night with you," Kim said. She was a great friend and was always there for her when she needed help.

"Ok Bitch, I'll see you when you get here," Re Re said, hanging up. She went to the bathroom and washed the dried up tears from her face. She pushed all thoughts of Money's lying ass to the back of her mind. She planned on enjoying her night with her girl.

(MEANWHILE – JUNE)

Four men sat inside a trap house passing around blunts, sipping codeine syrup, and drinking a few bottles of Ace of Spades, at the same time taking calls and making runs. This wasn't a nickel and dime trap house. They wasn't moving nothing less than a half a key. There was a knock at the door. Lil Mans, the runner, got up to answer. He peaked through the blinds and saw Cash's top hitter, June, with two other men standing outside.

"Open the door, Lil Nigga," June said. Lil Mans looked over to Drew.

"Drew, June at the door."

"Man, he knows better than coming over without calling. That's against the rules. Ask him what the fuck he wants," Drew yelled.

"What you want?" he asked with fear in his voice.

"Cash told me to stop by and check on shit," he replied.

"We can't open this door without a call from Cash."

"Look Pussy, Imma call Cash right now, but when he tell you to open this door, I'm gone push yo shit in for acting like you don't know who I am," June said, reaching in his pockets, grabbing his phone, and faking to dial Cash's number. Lil Mans open the door, stepping to the side to let them in.

"Naw, Big Homie, you ain't gotta do all that."

Drew heard the door open and called Lil Mans, "Who the fuck told you…" were his last words before Bullet put a hot one in his forehead. His body dropped to the floor, lifeless. June grabbed Lil Mans from behind in a headlock, placing one of his 9s to his noggin. The third man tried reaching for the assault rifle on the table, but it was too late, and he was beaten to the draw. Kutta aimed and hit him three times in the chest. He fell back into his seat on the couch. The fourth man was so high he just stood there surprised before reaching for his gun.

"Hands up or you next," Kutta yelled. He threw his hands in the air.

"Walk to me," Kutta instructed. Bullet took the revolver off him.

"Who else in here?" June asked Lil Mans, pushing him to the ground.

"Nobody, just us."

"Ok then, I'm gone give you one chance to tell me where the work at," June said.

"Don't tell them shit," the other men yelled. He wasn't dumb with his high blown. He understood they were dead men. There was no way they were leaving them alive after showing their face.

"Oh, we got a tough one," June said walking over to him. "When I die Imma die just like you, a soldier." June placed his 9 to his forehead and without hesitation he squeezed the trigger, blowing his brains all over Kutta's face.

"Fuck," Kutta yelled, wiping his face. After witnessing three of his friends get killed, Lil Mans was gone try to save his own life.

"The work upstairs in the room on the left under the bed. The money in the other room in the same place," Lil Mans said in one breath. Kutta and Bullet ran upstairs, guns ready to look for the stash.

"Man, you gone kill me anyways?" Lil Mans asked with pleading eyes.

"Ya, Lil Nigga, it's the number one rule of the streets, no witnesses," he said and pulled the trigger giving him one to the dome. He laid on the floor and the flat position. He hated this part of the game. The boy wasn't no older than 14. He just happened to be in the wrong place at the wrong time. Bullet and Kutta came downstairs with three duffle bags in hand.

"Jack fucking pot," Kutta said with a smile on his face. They all put their hoodies back on and left, hopping in a stolen car before making a clean getaway.

(HOURS LATER – JUNE)

June and his team were on the south side of Chicago outside another one of Cash's traps. This one would be difficult to rob. In about five minutes, the door to the house would open and four men would walk out, clinching anywhere from 100 to 500 Gs. Two of the men would be strapped with Mac 11, making sure the money got to its destination. The other men would be holding the money bags. Their plan was the same as before, June would hop out of his car for them to recognize him, and in the split second they looked away, Kutta and Bullet would ambush them with AKs. They were on the side of the house now, waiting to hear his voice. Another two minutes went by before they came walking out. June waited until they walked down the stairs before hopping out of the car. When they heard the car door open, everyone looked his way.

"What up, Folks," he yelled, throwing up the tre's. Just seeing him throw up the set, they let their guard down.

"Them treys," one of them yelled back. Kutta hit the corner. Ack-Ack-Ack-Ack-Ack-Ack-Ack. He discharged his weapon knocking them to the ground. June pulled out his two 9s with extended clips and aimed at the house, firing rounds to stop anyone from coming out. He shot out the windows. Bullet fired 10 slugs in the bodies on the ground. They grabbed the bags off the dead bodies before stepping over them. Kutta turned around and put five more rounds in each body to make sure they were dead before running and hopping in the car. June pulled off and someone came rushing out shooting, but they were down the block with another good lick. June understood there was a lot of work that needed to be done, but for now he would take his victory. An hour later it was 6 in the morning, and they were still counting up the money. At the first house, they got 250 bandz and five keys. At the second house, they came away with half a mil in cash.

"Man, good looking, June," Bullet said shaking up with Kutta.

"Hell ya, my nigga, good looking out," Kutta added.

"Look we all gone take $250,000 a piece, Imma keep the five birds for myself, y'all got a problem with that?" June asked.

"Hell naw," they replied simultaneously.

"Shit, it was yo lick. I'm happy with what I get. Shit, I'm hungry not dumb," Bullet said and they laughed, but he wasn't joking.

"Look now, y'all niggas can't be running around blowing this cash right away. It's gone bring heat on us we don't need right now. We gotta think smart, that way we could live to spend this and the million we gone make, y'all understand?" He wanted to make sure they didn't endanger his plans.

"Ya, we with you bro, on Dave," Kutta said, and Bullet just shook his head.

"Ok then, this most of the team and y'all gone meet everybody else later, we all we got. All I ask for is loyalty, and Imma make us rich, y'all with that?"

"You know it, Big Bro."

"No lie," Bullet added.

"Then let's get this money." They sat around smoking blunts for another hour before Bullet and Kutta went home. June called Kim, letting her know he'd be home tonight. He needs to get the five keys to Fat Boy. He was going let Fat Boy move them and split the money 50/50. That way Fat Boy ate as well. He didn't plan on being selfish. He wasn't like Cash; he wanted his whole team to be full.

(12:00 A.M. IN CHICAGO, CASH)

"What the fuck you mean somebody hit the spot?" Cash yelled in the phone. "You said what Nigga? I'm sending somebody over right now," he added, hanging up.

"Damn." He just lost a little under a million dollars in one fucking night. The messed up part was, he had eight funerals to plan. The person responsible knew a lot about his team. He wondered if it could be an inside job, but quickly decided none of his people was dumb enough to try him. The shit Money said struck a nerve. Maybe his brother was behind this. He needed to give this serious thought before making a move on family. They had limits and wouldn't come after each other, but that didn't rule him out. No harm came his way Only his money and solders lives were taken. That would be Money's approach at waging war on him. He wouldn't spare him if he was behind this. He didn't want people thinking he was playing games. It was time to send a message that he wasn't to be fucked with. He wanted everyone still alive at his spots murder for lacking. He picked up his phone and called his homie. Once he picked up, Cash said, "Send the service team to the spots that got hit today," and hung up. Niggas need to be on point at his spot or get killed. He didn't know who he was at war with, but once he found out, he would bring them to their knees.

Chapter 18

MONEY, TWO DAYS LATER

oney was busy getting his dreadlocks retwisted at the shop, when Re Re called for the fifth time. "Look, ma I'm sorry, but I can't keep doing this," he answered.

"But why?" Re Re cried. She didn't understand. She played her part, never doing anything to upset him. She sucked his dick whenever he called. She was the perfect mistress and gave her heart to his selfish ass.

"Look Ma, don't get me wrong, I got feelings for you, but I cant keep doing this to my relationship. It ain't right." He didn't wanna hurt her; that wasn't his intention. They were supposed to have a one-night stand. The day she gave him head, he never planned on falling for her, but he did. That was his reason for ending the relationship. Things with Angel and Kia were great. The head was amazing, but not worth losing everything.

"Please don't do this. I love you," she begged. He felt horrible on the inside, but wanted to be true to his girls.

"Look, Re Re, I'm sorry, I really am, but I gotta end this before it gets outta hand, Ma," he said.

"But what about me? What about my feelings?" Re Re questioned. This was her worst nightmare. She was damaged beyond repair. How could he be so unsympathetic and just end things all of a sudden?

"Look, Ma, I'mma make sure you good. You won't need anything, Imma pay yo bills until you get on your feet."

"I don't want your money. I want you," she expressed.

"Look, you can't have me. What part of that you don't understand?" Money yelled, loosing his patience.

"You know what, fuck you nigga. I don't need shit from you," Re Re said, hanging up on him. He sat the phone on his lap, feeling horrible. He heard the pain in her voice, and it did nothing for his conscious. He couldn't wait to get outta this shop so he could smoke some loud to relax his mind.

(MEANWHILE – RE RE)

Re Re was laid out on the floor in her apartment. It was a mess from the fit she threw after ending the call with Money. The pain she felt was strange; she wasn't accustomed to her emotions being played with. She held a .44 revolver in her hands, thinking about suicide when her phone rang.

"What," she answered.

"Get in your car and come and see me," Money demanded.

"For what?" she asked. He couldn't keep playing games with her heart.

"Cause I miss you."

"Look, Money, I can't keep playing these games with…"

"You coming or not?" he asked, cutting her off.

"Ya," she said and hung up. She hated being addicted to him. He controlled her and he knew it. After taking a shower and getting dressed, she went to get her fix.

(TWO HOURS LATER)

Re Re came out the bathroom with a hot towel to wash Money's dick off after some of the best make up sex. She picked up his limp cock and washed it as he slept. She glared at the man who hurt her the most, and wanted to kill him to separate herself from the control he had over her. She took the .44 from her bag and stared at him, wishing she could blow his brains out, but her love and affection wouldn't allow her to. What would she do without his passion? She couldn't murder him because she would crave him the moment he was gone. She put the gun back before laying in his arms. He pulled her close and held her. While in his arms, she thought of a plan to make him hers. The feeling of being with him was driving her insane. She was willing to kill for him. Money kissed her neck and rolled her over on her back, getting on top of her and entering her goods.

She pulled him to her saying, "I love you."

He was lost inside her honey box and would say anything to get his nut off, even lie. "I love you too."

(JULY 1, TWO WEEKS LATER, KIA)

Kia just came back from Madison dropping off three keys of boy to her team. She didn't update Money on how fast they went through the work. Instead, she went to the connect and bought three keys with her own money, and would come away with 600 Gs a month. She paid her girls and one-eyed Larry 30 Gs a piece to keep it on the low. She really didn't know what came over her in the last month or so, but she's found it difficult to play as a team player. She wants to rule over everybody. She loved Angel and Money, and that would never change. But there's something about deceiving people that really turned her on. The fact that a person viewed her as a beautiful woman. They never saw it coming until it was too late. That alone was enough to make her cum. She saved over 900 bandz and after this month, she'd be worth 1.5 million, and she was just getting started. As long as she was with Money, she didn't have to spend a dime. She had big dreams, and Danjunema needed to be under her spell and willing to make her dreams come true, even if that meant fucking him. She was meeting him tonight at his hotel, where she would put her spell on him. They'd been texting for about three weeks now. She told him about her being in love with Money, but added he couldn't please her sexually. She lied about needing his sex, but only if he respected her relationship. Like most men, he didn't have a problem making an agreement that benefited him. She lied to Money and Angel about going to a family member's funeral. She hated misleading him, but her mind-set was fuck a nigga, money make me cum.

(LATER THAT NIGHT, KIA)

Kia sat at a table in Ruxbin, one of Chicago's many 5-star establishments. Across from her sat Danjunema. The place was closed down, and they were the only two dining there tonight. For the first time in 15 years, he turned her on. She saw him in a new light than before. At first he was a person taking away her power, now he is the key to her dreams. Once she got into his head, the world would be hers. The only thing she needed to do was play her cards right.

"So Kia, are you having a good time?" he asked, licking his lips seductively.

"Yes I am. I love how you laid everything out, making me feel as comfortable as possible."

"Only the best for you, my lady. There would be no other approach for someone so special. All these things are superficial. They mean nothing without you being here. This situation I have dreamed of, you coming willingly, it's a fantasy come true," he said sincerely.

She stared into his eyes. "Then I will cum willingly all over your dick tonight," she said. They had a few more drinks before heading to his room. On the ride up they made out aggressively while he played with her pussy up under her dress. His two bodyguards rode up with them, but they weren't paying them any attention. His power brought out her inner slut. Once the door opened to the elevator, they rushed to his room. As he tried to get the door open, Kia saw one of the finest men she'd ever laid eyes on walking down the hall. His dredlocks hung free down to his chest. She wasn't into light-skin niggas, but he could get it. Danjunema got the door open, and his two guards stopped the man. He was putting up a fight when she was pulled into the room.

(MEANWHILE – JUNE)

"Look Bro, I don't give a fuck what yo job is. Don't put yo hands on me if you ain't ready to die," June said, staring into his eyes, but the tall African didn't back down. June was off the shits, and wasn't about to back down either. Just as he drew his gun, Kim came up behind him, placing her hand on his shoulder.

"You don't mind letting us pass, do you Big Man?" she asked in a sexy tone. They both took their hands off their firearms and stared at her mesmerized.

"Nah, we don't," the tall one said, stepping aside letting them pass. June never took his eye off the tall dude.

"Come on Baby, this not the time or the place," Kim mumbled with her hand on his back, pushing him towards the elevator. Once they were inside and the doors closed, he grabbed her around her neck, pushing her to the wall.

"Don't you ever underestimate me again in front of anyone," he yelled, letting her go.

"I just don't wanna see anything happen to you," she yelled as tears flowed endlessly down her cheeks. He turned around and looked into her eyes. Her hair was pulled up off her face, showing her features. She was beautiful. He leaned in for a kiss, wiping her tears away.

"I'm sorry Ma, I didn't mean to hurt you. It's just killing me wondering who killed my brother." He'd been drinking Hennessy and Ciroc mixed, trying to take the pain away. Smoking blunt after blunt and drinking codeine had him outta his body.

"I know, Baby," she said, standing in front of him as the elevator door opened, stopping him from exiting.

"Baby, it's too dangerous for you to go riding around like this. Come back to the room with me," she pleaded through tears.

"It's my job to keep you on point, and right now, Baby, you lacking. What you tell me happen to niggas, that be lacking?" she asked, and he didn't wanna admit he wasn't on point, but Kim wasn't new to the game. He couldn't lie to her.

"What happens to niggas that be lacking?" she asked once again.

"They get the 30 clip," he replied.

"Then come back upstairs."

"Ok Ma," she pushed the button to go up and turned around and kissed him.

"I love you, Daddy," she said for the first time.

"I love you too" he replied before they made it to their floor. The two African men were guarding the room exit. He heard loud moans coming from the room. June tried to remember where he saw that woman before. Then it hit him, she was getting in a car with Money and his wife the day Killa got killed. He wonder who she was to Money? Was she somebody or just a hoe, he thought. Kim opened the door to their room. He walked in and sat down on the lazy boy chair, pulling out a pre-rolled blunt. Before he flamed it up, Kim went to put a towel under the door. He loved her because she always did what was best for him. Most niggas wouldn't fuck with her after what she did to her baby daddy, but he wasn't worried about her loyalty to the next nigga, because to him she was loyal. He felt the way Lil Wayne felt *"as long as it was before me and you".* He didn't give a fuck about her past. She came over and sat on his lap.

"I'm sorry Ma, no lie, I will never put my hands on you again," he said, taking a pull from his blunt and turning his head away, blowing out the smoke.

"I know, Daddy, you just going through it right now," she said playing with one of his dreads.

"That's no excuse, Ma. I don't care what a man going through. It's never ok to hit his woman, and I don't want you to ever let a man put his hands on you," he said exhaling a fat cloud of smoke.

"Baby, I been thinking about getting my baby back from my mom. We doing good and I can take care of her now," she said. He didn't think that was a good idea. They were knee deep in the game, and he couldn't live with himself if something happened to Baby Girl.

"Not yet, Ma. We got a lil more work to put in. Then we gone get her when it's safe. Right now I need you on point to be my eyes in the back of my head. You the only person I can trust right now," he expressed. The sad expression that crossed her face almost killed him.

"Ok Daddy," she said standing up in headed to the bathroom. A few minutes later, he heard the shower running. He prayed she wouldn't think he didn't want to meet her baby, because he did and even though he didn't meet her yet, he loved her baby girl because she was a part of her. The streets didn't play fair, and right now wasn't a time to have a kid around. He took off his clothes before walking in the bathroom. He stepped in the shower behind her. Just looking at her body his dick hardened. She stuck her ass back to feel his long cock. He rubbed the head between her ass cheeks. She let out a low moan when he smacked her ass nice and hard.

"Daddy, do that again." He smacked her ass again two more times.

"Shit, I love that shit," she said really loud. June got out of the shower.

"Where you going, Daddy?" she asked, but he didn't answer and continued to walk back to the room. A minute later, Kim turned the shower off and walked out of the shower coming in the bedroom looking mad as hell.

"Why would you…" she was saying before stopping in the middle of her sentence once she saw 12 inches of dick standing at attention.

"Tonight you gone be my slut and do everything Daddy say," he said in a cold voice, but it turned her the fuck on. She stood in the doorway not able to move.

"Ok Daddy," she said in a low tone.

"Now get on your knees and come to Daddy." She did as she was told. When she made it to the bed, he stood over her. She took a hold of his dick and put it in her mouth.

"Did I tell you to suck my dick yet?" he said as he smacked her across her face with his cock.

"Naw, I'm sorry Daddy," she said getting into it like him.

"Now you can suck this muthafuka until I nut as yo punishment," he told her as she put it back in her mouth. She loved to suck dick. The sound of her sucking and slurping him almost took him to the point of erupting, but before he did, he pulled out. She had some of the best head he ever received.

"Imma need you to bend that fat ass over the bed," he instructed.

"Daddy, I want you to cum in my mouth first," she said.

"What the fuck I say?"

She stood up and bent over the bed. He saw her pussy staring back at him. He went in headfirst eating her ass.

"Oh, shitttt, oh do that shit, Daddy," she moaned. "Eat this ass, Daddy," she added going crazy, her pussy was gone be nice and wet. "I'm cumin don't stop, Daddy," she yelled. She came all over his face and he licked it up before he stood up and slammed half of his dick into her. "Oh shit, give it all to me, Daddy," she said, throwing her ass back trying to get all his dick.

He smacked her ass, "Ya throw that ass back for me, Ma." She begin to push back long and hard taking all of his dick in.

"Just like that, Ma." They fucked like this for 20 minutes before he was getting ready to nut.

"You still want it in your mouth, Ma?" he asked slapping her ass.

"Yes Daddy! All over my face." He pulled out and she turned around dropping to her knees. He jagged his dick off as she talked dirty to him licking her lips at the same time.

"Cum for me, Daddy." Just as she got the words out he busted all on her face. Once most of the nut was on her, she took the head of his dick in her mouth and sucked on it until he couldn't take it anymore and pulled out. She begin to rub her hand over her face and licking the nut off her fingers. She definitely was his slut tonight. Once she was finished, she headed to the shower and he fell out on the bed.

"Ring!" he heard his phone going off. He went in his pockets, pulling it out along with his brother's phone.

"What's good, Bro?" he asked talking to Kutta.

"Just checking up on you, making sure you good."

"Ya, I'm good Lil Bro, good looking on checking," June said.

"Aight, loyalty," Kutta said and ended the call. Kutta called him every night to make sure he was good. That's why he fucked with him and Bullet; they reminded him of his brother. He turned his brother's phone on and went through his pictures. He really missed the lil nigga. After about five minutes of going through it, he came across a picture of Money and his wife with the bitch next door. It look like Killa was following them. What the fuck would Killa be following them for? He needed some answers and he knew where to get them.

Chapter 19

KIA, THE NEXT MORNING

*K*ia left the Ritz Carlton Hotel and called Money but didn't get an answer. A minute later he called her back. "What's good, Ma."

"What you doing?" she asked.

"Shit, riding around."

"Oh."

"Imma call you back," Money said rushing off the phone. Kia wasn't dumb; he was acting different lately. She worried he found out about her cheating or worse, making business deals behind his back.

"Ok, then I'll talk to you later," she said hanging up in his face. Her guilty conscious had her on edge. She didn't want to assume anything, but lately he'd been acting suspicious. She called Angel to see if he was only acting crazy with her.

"What's up, Bitch?" Angel asked, sounding a little too upbeat for this time of morning.

"Nothing. I gotta ask you a question," Kia said.

"What?"

"Has Money been acting funny?"

"Ya, girl" Angel said. She didn't understand what it was, but she thought he was cheating.

"Ok, so it's not just me," Kia said.

"Nah, it ain't. Do you think he cheating?" Angel asked, addressing the elephant in the room. Kia didn't know, and would do whatever to find out, but she would have to know for sure before she hurt Angel.

"Girl, why would he cheat on us, we too bad," Kia said throwing Angel off.

"Ya you right," Angel replied.

"Imma call you back."

"Ok, girl," Kia hung up and went shopping. She was gone find out what changed about him if it was the last thing she did.

(MEANWHILE – RE RE)

Re Re rode shotgun with Money to Chicago. Things were good between them. Money picked her up this morning to go shopping and spend some time with her. With him outta the game, he had more free time. Re Re felt good about their relationship. They had an understanding, and he would make time for her as well. Sofar he'd kept his word. With an hour ride ahead of them, she thought it would be fun to give him head on I-90.

(AN HOUR LATER - KIA)

Kia sat inside her car after putting her bags in the back seat, when she got the surprise of a lifetime - Money was walking holding hands with another woman. They looked happy, and that broke her heart. How could he do this to her, to them? Before she knew it, a tear escaped her eyes. She wiped it away, remembering her promise to never cry over a man. She watched them enter Grace Restaurant before she pulled off with a heavy heart. What would she tell Angel? How could she explain what she saw? She made up her mind she wouldn't make Angel suffer for their man's careless-ness. It was her job to protect her and she would, by any means.

Warm tears rolled down her face and into the corners of her mouth. She couldn't breathe and began to hyperventilate. The pain she felt was like no other; it was deeper than the surface. She felt it down to the bone. Her stomach began to turn, and she felt like she would vomit. She let the window down to get some air. The thought of confronting Money came to mind, but she quickly discarded that. The cost for breaking her heart could only be paid for with his life. The wheels in her mind came to life. She would use Danjunema to get rid of Money, and her and Angel could live happily ever after. She knew killing him would devastate Angel, and might bring her to the brink of death, but they would make it through it together. And for once she would have Angel to herself. She wiped the tear from her face before going to make a deal with Satan.

(FIVE HOURS LATER - MILWAUKEE)

Money pulled up to the house an hour ago. He dropped Re Re off after they spent a wonderful day together. She was really growing on him, and he had a soft spot in his heart for her. His emotions were all over: one minute he wanted to leave her alone, the next minute she was laying in his arms. He picked up his phone and called Angel, letting her know he was outside. They were going out on a date tonight. Kia was supposed to come along, but at the last minute canceled. So it would just be him and Angel. He thought about Kia and how she'd been acting lately. Something was different about her, he just didn't know what. Angel walked outta the house looking amazing, and he remembered how she stole his heart so many years ago. At that moment he knew Re Re could never compare to his first love. He needed to end things permanently this time. He got out and opened the door for his queen.

"Thanks, Daddy," she said, getting in the car. He hopped back in the driver's seat and pulled off.

"Daddy, let me see yo phone to play music. I broke my phone earlier," she asked, putting her hand out. Money went in his pocket and handed her his phone. She hooked it up and played their favorite song. She reached over and grabbed his hand. Money took his eyes off the road, looking at the love of his life. They stared in each other's eyes and Angel whispered, "I love you," putting a smile on his face.

"I love you too," he said pulling into a gas station. He ran in and grabbed some blunts and put $50 on the pump. After pumping the gas, he got in the car. The music wasn't playing and Angel's whole demeanor changed. Tears ran down her face and she threw his phone in his lap.

"Who the fuck is Re Re?" she asked wiping the tears from her eyes. "And why the fuck you got naked pictures of the bitch in yo phone?" she said pointing her finger in his face.

"Wha… wait Ma, I can explain," he said nervous. "Look I… I fucked up."

"You damn right you did," she said cutting him off. And slapping him and his face. "Nigga, I gave you everything, I held you down for five years. Five fucking years," she said holding up five fingers. "And this is how you repay me." She stopped yelling and broke down. "Me tho, Money, outta all people, me, what two bitches wasn't enough for you, huh?"

Money couldn't say anything. All he did was rub his finger through his hair.

"Take me home, Money," she spoke looking the other way. He started the car up and pulled off. He dropped Angel off without another word said between them two. Angel went inside while he sat in the car, trying to get his thoughts together. He was confused on whether he should go in and talk to her or give her space to think. He decided to talk to her. When he made it inside, Angel was laying on the bed face down, crying. He walked over and sat next to her, putting his hand on her back.

"Baby, I'm sorry," he whispered. "I fucked up and I can't take it back. I know that, but I can make it right. I will make it right. I just need another chance. Can you give me another chance?" he asked. Angel turned over, gazing into his eyes. She wanted to tell him to go to hell. But she couldn't, she needed him. Up until today she was at peace and comfortable with him. Right now she was in control of her fate. She didn't have to put herself through the torture of getting over him. She loved him with all her heart.

"You gotta end it right away," she said sitting up. Money got on his knees in front of her.

"Baby, it's done," he said rubbing her legs. She wrapped her arms around his neck and hugged him. He kissed her lips laying her on the bed in she held him close.

"Promise me you'll never leave," she said between the kiss.

"I'll never leave you, Ma," he said, standing up taking his shirt off. She sat up and ran her hands over his six-pack, looking up at his lovely eyes. There was no place she'd rather be than with him. No love like his, she knew she was addicted to his love. She just prayed he could fuck her into forgiving him.

(THE NEXT DAY)

Money woke up and made the trip to Beloit. Last night they made the decision to keep it a secret about his cheating. Angel didn't wanna hurt Kia, so she made Money agree to end his relationship with Re Re. He pulled up outside her apartment and took a second to get his thoughts together. He didn't wanna break her heart, but he wasn't about to lose his relationship over a peace of ass. He got out the car and knocked on the door. A moment later, Re-Re opened the door.

"Hi, Baby," she said letting him in. Money walked in and stood next to the door with his hands in his pocket, he looked down and he felt her eyes rolling over at him, but he didn't acknowledge her existence. She closed the door and stood in front of him.

"Is everything ok?" she asked. He sat silently, unable to look at her.

"I can't do this no more," he said looking at the floor. After a minute of silence, Re Re took a seat.

"The least you could do is tell me why," she said looking at the ceiling, doing the best job she could to hold back the tears.

"I got a family, Re Re," he said walking over to her. "This wasn't suppose to go this far." he said backing away from her. "I'm sorry Ma, I really am." He opened the door and walked out. He heard the door lock behind him. He felt like a piece of shit at the moment.

Who was he to play with somebody's heart? He got in the Bentley and pulled away.

Re Re heard a knock at the door, she pulled the .44 bulldog from her head, and put it under the bed. She opened the door without looking, thinking it was Money.

"What the fuck you want," she yelled before being sacked in the face with an agonizing force. She fell in the house and a pistol slammed against her face again. Her eyes filled with blood, she heard the door close and lock as she struggled to get back on her feet. Blood was pouring from her nose and mouth.

"Money, why?" she asked, then she heard a female laugh.

"Bitch, you gone wish this was Money. At least he might show mercy," the woman said kicking her back to the ground.

"So you like fucking him, Bitch?" the voice asked before delivering a kick to her stomach.

"Did you, Bitch?" she asked again, pushing her.

"No, we ended things tonight," she said hoping to save her life. She felt a hand wrap around her hair pulling her to her feet. The woman punched her in the face, and she crashed to the carpet.

"Oh my god!" Re Re cried out. The woman kicked her in the ribs with the tip of her boots then clunked her upside the head with the side of her pistol. She aimed the gun at her face.

"Please don't hurt me, I didn't do anything," Re Re continued to cry.

"You didn't do anything, huh?" she asked. Boc!

A devastating force slammed into her stomach, and a burning sensation spread throughout her upper body and she struggled to breath. Boc!Boc!

Re felt the next two bullets hit her chest and she rolled around in pain. The woman stood over her and aimed the barrel at her face.

"I hope the dick was worth dying for," she said firing the weapon.

Boc!

She stepped over Re Re's dead body and left the house. One down, one to go.

(TWO WEEKS LATER)

Over the last two weeks, Kia thought about Money cheating. Her heart split between wanting revenge and not wanting to kill him. Money sat on the passenger side as Kia drove to meet a buyer. Being the owner of the hottest nightclub in the city made it effortless to find new business partners. Angel knew everyone by name, and Money picked the people he felt could be trusted. He picked five men. They were headed downtown to make a sell. The customer they were meeting ordered three keys at 80 bandz a piece. They were making 30 Gs off this meeting. They pulled up to the strip mall. Money hopped in the back seat before they picked the man up. He didn't believe in letting a person sit behind him when doing business. They could easily blow his brains out and take everything.

"What's good?" Drew asked, hopping in the car.

"Hey," Kia said back.

"Where the cash at?" Money asked. Drew handed over his duffle bag, and Money skimmed over the currency, making sure it was correct.

"Here," Money said, handing over the bricks. Kia dropped him off at his car then pulled over to Mickey D's where Money got in the front seat.

"This shit hot. We gotta get a front business to sell this shit out of," Money said.

"Like a clothing store?" Kia asked, pulling off.

"Hell yeah, street niggas gone fit right in. We gone talk to Angel about helping you set that up, cause ain't shit happening at the club." Kia laughed, she knew Angel wasn't gone have that shit. She loved that club. Money laid back in his seat.

"Kia, I wanna thank you for always having my back, and I know you have a hard time trusting me with the connect, but I would never do anything to hurt you," he said sincerely. "We all we got in these streets and we gotta protect each other and trust each other," he added. She felt her body temperature rise and her emotions flipped. She despised how he was acting like everything was fine when just two weeks ago, he was with the next bitch, smiling and having a good time. Now he was asking for trust.

"Ok whatever, Money," she said rolling her eyes.

"What's all that for?" he asked.

"Nothing, Boy," she said trying not to take it there with him.

"If you got something on yo mind, get it off," he said looking over at her, but she kept her attention on the road.

"I'm cool," she said angrily. Over the last few weeks, he noticed a difference in her; he couldn't put his finger on it. She had become controlling and wanted to make all the moves herself.

"Look Kia, I don't know what yo problem been the last few weeks, but you gotta get it together, cause that attitude getting old." She looked at him with rage in her eyes, but when she spoke she acted sad.

"I'm sorry, Daddy, I just been feeling some type of way about my people passing," she said, telling a lie.

"I know, but you can't take it out on the family, you gotta remember we all we got. Don't let nothing come between that," he said putting his hands on her lap.

"I love you Girl, and I got you."

"I love you too, Daddy," she said pulling up to the house. Money stepped out of the car and grabbed the cash.

"Oh Daddy, I forgot I have a meeting with the connect right now, so I'm gone be home later ok?"

"Cool, love you," Money said.

"Money, you got anything you wanna tell me?" Kia asked.

"Why you asked that?" he questioned.

"I don't know. I guess you been acting kind of funny lately."

"Nah Ma. I'm good. Don't worry about me."

"Ok then, Daddy. I love you."

"Love you too." He said closing the door. Kia pulled off upset. He was acting like he wasn't a cheater and like everything was fine. She still hadn't told Angel what happened and had no plan on doing so. She made her mind up; he had to go. She gave him two weeks to confess, and he didn't, which confirmed her belief he never loved her. In that time, she went through many stages before she turned into something so horrible. Her case proved there was a thin line between love and hate.

(MEANWHILE – JUNE)

June observed Kia the last two weeks. She was really into some shit. Over that time he found out she was moving hella work, and if he wasn't mistaken, the African was her connect, and Money her man. She was fucking the African as well. He also learned from Tez the night Killa got shot, he had a few words with Money inside the club. Tez believed Money shot him. That would be the reason Killa was following him, to murder the nigga. June decided tonight was Money's last night alive. He had to make it happen for his lil brother. If there was any chance he was behind his brother's murder, he had to go.

(LATER THAT NIGHT)

Things were going as planned for Kia. Just as she thought, Danjunema became her bitch and didn't even know it. He thought he was in control, but he gave his power to her weeks ago. She training him to follow her instructions just as you train your dog. When he did something wrong, she punished him, and when he did something right, she rewarded him. She called Money to tell him she would be home later before exiting the bathroom to give Danjunema his reward. She stood in the doorway naked, in all of her glory, before walking over to the bed where Danjunema was laid. She stepped on the mattress and stood over him. She closed her eyes and squatted down putting her pussy on his face. She begin to grind her pussy lips over his face and, taking ahold of his head. The only way she could get off was him eating her pussy, and like a gentleman, he let the lady go first. After an hour of sex, Kia picked up her phone and called Angel as planned. She didn't want her in the house when Danjunema's men came. The phone rang three times before going to voicemail. She tried again, but didn't get an answer. She shook Danejunema, waking him from his sleep.

"You got to call it off," she yelled.

"Call it off why?" he asked, confused.

"Because she's still there!" she screamed. Her heart skipped a beat and the only thing she could think of was Angel.

"Ok! Ok! Relax," he said picking his phone up off the nightstand to call off the hit, but got no answer. He tried again, but still no answer.

"It's too late," he said trying to hug her. She pushed him off her and raced to put on her clothes.

"Kia, there's nothing you can do now," he said in his heavy accent. Kia didn't hear a word of it as she rushed out the door.

(MEANWHILE – MONEY)

Money came in the house after going to Western Union to send the money for Re Re's funeral. He thought about the call he had received earlier from Re Re's sister. She told him her body was found inside her house yesterday. She'd been dead for over a week. The police was holding back information and would only tell her it was being investigated as a homicide. When he walked in the house, he heard music playing upstairs. When he made it up the stairs he heard Angel yell, "Money, come here."

When he walked in, she was lying in bed naked, her phone was vibrating on the nightstand, but they didn't hear it because their favorite song was playing. Mary J Blidge sang her heart out.

"Come here, Daddy," she said. Money climbed on the bed between her legs. Kissing her, he looked in her passion-filled eyes.

She stared in his eyes and hungrily kissed him back. She could feel the tip of his growing cock pressing between her legs. He pulled himself away from her and undressed. Angel watched him as she wet her finger and started massaging her juicy cunt. He looked at her with a devilish smile and made his way down to her wet pussy. He separated her labia with his fingers and placed his tongue on her clit. She couldn't stop moaning. Every flick of his tongue brought her closer to orgasm. Finally she couldn't take any more; she wanted him inside her. Angel turned around and pressed her ass against his cock. She could feel the head of his dick nestled at the entrance of her vagina. She guided him into her moistness. He slid in inch by inch until their bodies touched. Their favorite song played on repeat.

"Make love to me Daddy, like it's the last time." He worked his cock nice and slow. The sensation of his large dick moving slowly inside her drove her to a frenzy. His lips wandered down her neck, and her nipples hardened as his fingers played with them. She ran her finger up her thigh and around his balls. In perfect unison they thrust against each other. His fingers rubbed her and she screamed as the sensation took her over the edge. The spasms of her climaxing made him nut. And they collapsed, sighing in pleasure, totally spent. After a minute, Money put his boxers on, turned on the T.V., and the security channel popped on. Three heavily armed men entered their house. The first man placed his index finger to his lips, signaling for them to remain quiet. He motioned for them to slip up, and crept up the stairs with a assault riffles clutched in his hand.

"Shhh," Money said putting his finger on his lips. "Get up and go in the bathroom." Angel looked at the security camera, her chest raised and fell as she began to sob and looked to Money for assistance.

"What about you?" she whispered in a nervous frenzy. Money reached under the bed and came out with two 9s and handed one to Angel.

"What am I suppose to do?" she asked.

"Calm down and go into the bathroom, that gun is in case they get to you, now go."

"I love you," she said as she tiptoed to the bathroom with tears in her eyes.

"I love you too," he mouthed to her before she shut the door. Just as he glanced at the T.V., one man rushed into the room with his M16 in his hand. Money gripped his hammer and raised up from the side of the bed, putting four rounds in his chest. He stood up and grabbed the assault riffle as the man laid in a puddle of blood. His body spasmed for a few seconds before his soul left the earth. Money crept to the other end of the hallway. The second shooter made his way up the stairs, AK-47 locked and loaded. He heard music coming from a room. He looked down and saw his brother Gero's body laying in a pool of blood.

"Gero," Chipo said putting his gun down and knelt next to him. Without hesitating Money raised the M16 and fired. Boc! Boc!

The first bullet burned through the back of Chipo's head, sending a chunk of hair out the left side of his check. The second bullet ripped through his neck and he folded over his brother's body.

That's when all hell broke out. A man came behind him firing 20 rounds, Money ducked down as the bullets ripped through everything in the hallway. A bullet went through the wall and hammered him in the back knocking his firearm out his hand. The shooter ran towards Money, but two bullets struck him down, one ripped through his shoulder and the other through the back of his head. Angel walked up the hallway gun still in hand. Money rolled over in pain. Angel stood over him aiming the barrel at his face. Her face was puffy, her eyes were red and her body was trembling.

"What you doing, Ma?" he asked, his heart dropped into his stomach.

"You couldn't just walk away?" Angel said crying hysterically. "You had to pay for the bitch funeral, after I killed her for us," she yelled. Money couldn't believe what he was hearing.

"Angel calm down, and get some help. I'm losing a lot of blood Baby." Angel laughed and wiped away the tears, a smile spread across her face.

"Come on Daddy, be a man, I need to see you stand tall before you die. That way I'll always remember you as a stand up nigga," she joked. Money felt himself passing out from all the blood he was losing. He began to see angels and demons fight over his soul. Angel smacked the shit outta him, bringing him back to life for a moment.

"Angel, I'm sorry I never meant for this to happen," he said. Angel broke down crying. She couldn't bring herself to pull the trigger. Money was fading in and out. He watched as demons pulled his soul away.

"Freeze! Put the gun down," he heard someone yell. He opened his eyes and saw a police officer aiming an automatic at Angel's head. She smiled at him, and turned towards the officer with the gun raised.

Boc!

Angel body drops slamming to the floor with a Nicky sized hole in her forehead. Money laid on the ground looking into her lifeless eyes. *Sometimes I can't believe that you are with me, there's nobody lucky as me, so I get on my knees to make sure that he, knows that I'm grateful for what he gave me.* The words from their beloved song played, as he took his last look at the love of his life, before the demons pull his soul away from his body to spend an eternity in the underworld.

(4 A.M. THE SAME NIGHT)

Kia pulled up to the house, there were cops scattered around their home. The house was taped off. She stepped outta her car and ran up the driveway.

"What's going on, officer?" Kia asked looking around.

"Why, do you live here, Miss?"

"Yes, I do, what happened?"

"I'm sorry to be the one to inform you of this, but there are five people, four men and a woman deceased inside." The last words she heard before passing out was "woman deceased." When she woke up the next morning, she was inside a hospital room alone. She sat up in bed just as Danjunema walked in.

"Are you ok?" he asked.

"Do I fucking look ok to you?" she said with murder in her eyes.

"Just get the hell out, get out now!" she yelled. The look of disappointment on his face she never saw before, but right now she could care less. Her life would never be the same again. How could it? She just lost the two people she loved most. All she could think about was, did Angel cry or beg for her life? Why did God always bring pain to her? She would never know. But from this day forward she would never love again.

"I'm sorry about what happen," Danjunema said, walking out the door. Right now, all she wanted to do was cry. Tears rolled out of her eyes heavily, but she was laughing, she felt grief for losing Angel. But emotions wouldn't be wasted on Money because what was done was done. She was devastated by his betrayal and blamed him for Angel's death. He had every chance there was to confess and he didn't. She refused to be in love with a liar, but was addicted to his love. Too addicted for him to live and her to go without it. If he was alive, she would always run to him for a fix. The choice she made was tough, but being misused and mistreated was tougher. She fought so hard not to fall in love with him because her heart couldn't take it. Tears rolled down her face and she looked to the prince of darkness, hoping he'd give her answers. She wiped the snot and tears off her face with the back of her hand. She wanted to just sit around, but she needed to take care of business first. She needed to get outta this room before police showed up asking questions she didn't want to answer at this time. She got outta bed, retrieving her clothes off the chair and putting them on. She took out her iPhone and called a cab. The show still had to go on and money still needed to be made. It took 20 minutes before she got the call that her cab was outside. Her mind was all screwed up and her feelings were all over the place. Why her? Why did this happen to her? She needed some time away.

"How are you doing?" the cab driver asked.

"I'm fine," she lied.

"Where are you headed?" he asked.

She gave him the address to their home. She had to make one last stop there, and then she was leaving town for a while. She wanted to get away from the hell her life had become. But what about the money and the power she demanded so badly? None of that seemed to matter right now. They pulled up to the house, and she paid the driver, then stepped out. She looked at the house. There was still crime scene tape around it, but the police were gone. She stepped in the house and got goose bumps. She almost passed out again, just being inside the house. She made her way to the living room and removed the picture of King David on the wall, blocking the safe. She entered the combination and snatched it open, and there was no surprise when she found stacks of money. Through her expert eyes, she approximate the money being well over 2 million, and a smile crossed her face. She ran up the stairs to grab some duffle bags. When she walked into their old room, it was a mess. There were bullet holes in the walls and two bloodstains on the floor. She rushed back downstairs and start unloading the money. She headed to the garage and took the extra set of keys to the Bentley before loading the money into the car, pulling off. She pulled up to her house and once she got inside, she began packing her money into more duffle bags, putting them inside the Bentley. She had no idea where she was going, but wanted to get away. She pulled off and hopped on the freeway.

(MEANWHILE – JUNE)

June waited outside Money's house until Kia showed up 10 minutes ago and began loading bag after bag of what he assumed to be money before pulling off. He followed her as she hopped on the highway. His mind wondered to last night. Shit got crazy. He knew there was no turning back now; he had to play things out. Shit was a lot deeper than what he first thought. This bitch was a pretty savage!

TO BE CONTINUED...